ANNIHILATION

PIOTR SZEWC

Annihilation

A NOVEL

Translated by Ewa Hryniewicz-Yarbrough

DALKEY ARCHIVE PRESS

Originally published as *Zagłada* by Czytelnik Publishers (Warsaw, Poland) in 1987. The following translation is the revised version the author prepared for the French, Italian, and American editions.

Library of Congress Cataloging-in-Publication Data
Szewc, Piotr, 1961-
[*Zagłada.* English]
Annihilation : a novel / Piotr Szewc ; translated by Ewa Hryniewicz-Yarbrough. — 1st ed.
I. Title.
PG7178.Z39Z2513 1993 891.8'5307—dc20 93-18996
ISBN 1-56478-034-1

First Edition

Partially funded by grants from The National Endowment for the Arts and The Illinois Arts Council.

Dalkey Archive Press
4241 Illinois State University
Normal, IL 61790-4241

Printed on permanent/durable acid-free paper and bound in the United States of America.

ANNIHILATION

We are on Listopadowa, the second street crossing Lwowska. In one of the tiny backyards close to the intersection, Mr. Hershe Baum is standing near the house and feeding pigeons perched on his arm. Here they are called Persian butterflies. Isn't it a beautiful name? In all likelihood they were brought from Persia. But is that certain? We won't be able to verify it. Data, documents, and credible explanations are unavailable. Supposedly the pigeons can fly for many hours at a height that makes them invisible to the human eye. But since we received this information from a merely casual acquaintance, we cannot vouch for its accuracy. We haven't been interested in such matters. It is beyond doubt, however, that Mr. Hershe Baum's pigeons are highly valued by local pigeon breeders. One often sees buyers of his birds. Now, at the peak of the season, the pigeons draw high prices.

A horse-drawn wagon loaded with sacks passes by. It's only logical to assume it carries grain—a flour mill is located on Listopadowa, and the cart is going in that direction. As our eyes follow the cart, the sun, reflected off a window that someone is opening, blinds us. Soon, through the half-opened window, an extended hand pours the contents of a chamber pot. The whole scene takes only a few seconds. Before we can notice it, the pigeons, scared by the clatter of the wagon, fly off Mr. Hershe Baum's arm. And the hens cackle loudly when the contents of Kazimiera M's pot lands on them. It was Kazimiera M who poured what was in the pot out the window. Although it's warm, Kazimiera M carefully closes the window. For a moment we see her white gown through the windowpane.

Most likely she went to sleep late, and now, after she has emptied the pot, she will want to lie down for at least half-an-hour or so. Sleep is best the morning after a busy night. To keep the sun out, Kazimiera M decides to draw the curtains. Even if we wanted, we couldn't peek into her apartment. So let's allow Kazimiera M a well-deserved rest.

Mr. Hershe Baum, who until this minute was standing near the house, shoos away the pigeons clamoring for more grain and ambles into the street. He picks up an apple, one of many scattered in front of the house, and standing outside the opened gate, he brings the apple to his mouth. It has a nice tart taste. With his free hand, he shades his eyes. He contemplates the sun, which has already reached the trees behind the brewery. For the last few days the sun has been unusually bright.

Mr. Hershe Baum calls his wife out of the apartment. Now, shading their eyes, both look at the sun. It takes only a moment. Then Mrs. Baum drops her hand and returns to the apartment. Her husband closes the gate and follows. From here we can see a narrow ribbon of brown smoke escape from the chimney pipe. Unstirred by the slightest breeze, it rises weightlessly, straight up. And since we are still on Listopadowa, we see small particles of burned paper glide through the air, settle on leaves and grass, then rise again and soar above the trees. Soon the chimney pipe of the Baums' cast-iron stove starts spewing out lighter colored clouds of smoke, which the pigeons, agitated by Mr. Baum, immediately scatter. If it weren't for the unquestionable presence of a mild smell of burning, as well as the soot and ashes that cover the leaves, nobody would suspect that a few minutes ago smoke was emerging from the chimney.

Those few minor events most likely will not influence future events universally considered most significant. The minor events will vanish in the turmoil surrounding more important events and will not be salvaged by memory or photographs. They belong to the past that isn't studied—they are question marks left by each successive generation. Like burned paper, they, together with similar facts and circumstances, will turn to dust scattered in time.

In a week or two or a month Mr. Hershe Baum, the owner of the fabric store that we'll soon have a chance to see, will not even remember last night's nightmarish dream, which he didn't expect or deserve. In his dream the town was flooded. Human heads floated in the water—his own, his wife Zelda's, and their five children's—surely the heads of half the people in town. Strangely enough the water was clear, bloodless, and instead of grass, algae were visible under the surface.

For the foreseeable future we shouldn't ignore all those minor events that are occurring before our eyes. They not only form a unique background for those most important events but presumably they also influence them and will influence them in some way. Mr. Baum's dream, for example, is an extremely bad omen for him.

In the meantime Kazimiera M appears again. She has drawn the curtains apart. Dreamily she opens the window, then raises her hands and stretches. For a moment she freezes, yet right away we see the rhythmic movement of her breasts beneath the nightgown. She twists her long brown hair around her fingers, lifts it above her head, and lets it slowly fall onto her shoulders and back.

At the same time, Mr. Hershe Baum, the mercer, walks into Lwowska and heads for the market square. He must be hurrying to his store to open it on time. Kazimiera M, still standing within our vision, combs her hair at the window, while Attorney Walenty Danilowski slowly closes the swinging door to Rosenzweig's tavern.

We are at the edge of the market square, where Lwowska begins. One of us takes a picture. The photographer can shoot at will. Only the width of the lens curbs his freedom. The world is frozen for a fraction of a second. What do we see after the film is developed? Unnatural, somewhat grotesque figures of passersby and of a bicyclist. Two policemen are entering the tavern. The swinging door hasn't quite closed. Through the crack we see a raised hand holding a beer stein.

Many years later someone will leaf through an old photo album. But something will be amiss: the photographs didn't record details, seemingly insignificant, yet important and interesting for the person who looks at the pictures. What we can see now from close up will be invisible or unidentifiable in the photo: the photo doesn't reveal the grimace of confusion or surprise on the face of the bicyclist.

Unfortunately, the photo omits other details as well.

It is impossible to say whether it is Attorney Danilowski who is holding the beer stein in Rosenzweig's tavern. Future close-up techniques would prove that the hand indeed belongs to this gentleman. The cut and the color of the cuff (dark green check) and the number (two) of the buttons would testify to that.

Something else is in the picture.

In the left-hand corner a shapeless spot is visible. Standing in the market square, we know that it is a little black-haired girl. Since we are witnessing the events captured by the photo, we see more than people who will be leafing through the photo album over half-a-century later.

They will detach the pictures and examine them closely. And what will they see? Here someone raises a beer stein or a glass; here someone bikes; here a woman stands, her back turned, her head bent to the side. In the upper left-hand corner a grey spot shows—what could it be? Perhaps clothes hung out to dry? Perhaps a child? They don't know. Frustrated, they stick the photo back in the slits on the page and close the album. For a while longer the images remain in their minds, but we can be sure that those images will soon be forgotten.

The policemen whom we saw entering Rosenzweig's tavern are now comfortably sprawled out on the benches alongside a large table. They comment on last night's events—in fact there weren't any events worth their while—and now and then they wet their lips with beer foam. The sight of the policemen drinking beer should surprise no one: it's early morning and they have the right to feel tired after night duty. As a matter of fact, they aren't here by themselves, although the tavern is still almost empty. They glance at Attorney Danilowski, sitting nearby, and time after time wink wryly at each other. But Mr. Walenty Danilowski seems not to notice and orders another beer. When he visits the tavern, during its least crowded hours, he tries to forget his ailing liver, which to his dismay often demands a special diet. According to his doctor's advice, the attorney should abstain from alcohol. But he enjoys the beer served by the owner of the tavern, beer which is justly famous for going straight to the head.

Both policemen are young and, as usual, ready to crack

coarse jokes. That isn't surprising: during the hours of their night duty, they have an opportunity to observe many things never seen by most residents. Attorney Danilowski decides not to pay attention to the policemen, to ignore their presence as far as possible. "Did Kazimiera remember to give the attorney something stronger? A glass of slivovitz to cheer up." After saying this, one of the policemen, Antoni Wrzosek, lifts his beer stein towards Mr. Danilowski as if to drink a toast. In response the attorney emphatically clears his throat and takes a noisy sip of his beer. Let them make such remarks somewhere else in town—in the street maybe but not here, for god's sake, not here!

Offended by this apparent lack of tact, Attorney Danilowski leaves the unfinished beer and, vigorously pushing the door, exits the tavern. Maybe he's returning home. Or maybe he's going to his office since it's his habit to start work early.

For the policemen, for Mr. Hershe Baum, for Kazimiera M, for Attorney Danilowski, and for those now present at the market square—as well as for all the other residents—their town in its microcosmic scale is the model of the universe: with the arm of the river encircling it to the south, with its mesh of streets, its shrines, and its orchards. The Town Hall, the church, and the market square form the center where the ritual of life is enacted. We can assume that all those people are wholeheartedly convinced that they live in the *true* center. Other towns, rivers, and unknown people, separated from them by time and space, are like ripples made by a pebble that someone has thrown in the water.

As early as five in the morning, the sharp rays of the July sun turn the market square into an arena for a spectacular display of chiaroscuro. Filtered through leafy branches, the rays cast vibrant and unreal images onto the pavement. Where the images vibrate, the shadows of houses, stores, and market stalls blend into dark rectangles crowned with roof points. Similar images can be seen on the walls and windows of houses, stalls, and stores overgrown with vines. And such images can be seen now, although the clock struck five a long time ago. *(A long time ago for whom? How long?)*

In the door to one of the stores we see Mr. Hershe Baum. A sign saying FABRIC STORE hangs above the door and the window. The market square isn't busy yet. Occasionally Mr. Hershe Baum gestures or says something to invite passersby to visit the store. What a selection of fabrics! Mr. Baum is extremely pleased with the last shipment he received from Lvov. The open shutters display a sampling of fabrics.

The southern wall of Mr. Baum's store—like the walls of other buildings and stores—is overgrown with vines. They stretch across the roof and fall over the windows on the opposite side. We can hear sparrows chirping and hopping among the creepers.

Mr. Baum enters the store and disappears into its dark interior. For a moment, through the window, we see his head before the shelves of fabric.

We are accompanied by the ubiquitous smell of rotting wood and dank boards, a smell which is trapped in the market square.

Just now, Attorney Danilowski is passing Saint Augustine's Church. He takes a watch out of his pocket. It's three minutes to seven.

Attorney Danilowski isn't in a hurry; he has a lot of time. It won't take more than twenty minutes to get to his office. According to the blue sign posted on the door, the office isn't supposed to open until eight. In a little store opposite the church the attorney buys mints. He puts one into his mouth and stuffs the rest, wrapped in paper, into his pocket. He's expecting a visit from a certain tenant who lives near Zwierzyniec.

The tenant announced his impending arrival by letter. The attorney has already reviewed the case once—it's quite common and rather uninteresting. Today, his client writes, he will hear new details which will supposedly throw more light—but will they really?—on the progress of the case.

Unfortunately, this is not the greatest way to spend the morning. The attorney would like to return to Rosenzweig's tavern for another beer, or stop by at Kazimiera M's, even though the time isn't convenient. The latter option is more enticing, but he doesn't turn back. He merely puts another mint into his mouth.

It looks like the day will be hot—probably as hot as the past few days. Dew still covers the grass. The morning is beautiful. The dome of the church glistens copper gold. The parish priest closes the door of the sacristy and walks toward the presbytery. A droshky passes the church. The cabman whips the horses and the droshky disappears into the nearest cross street. A dog that was barking stops for a while but soon starts again, louder this time and closer.

The two policemen leave Rosenzweig's tavern. The younger of them wipes beer foam off his mustache. The policemen's shoes shine in the morning sun although at night they should have gathered at least a thin layer of dust. Their heels rhythmically kick the pavement. In the general din their steps sound like the measured ticking of a clock.

The policeman who has just wiped his mustache asks one of the passersby to tell him the time. "It's almost seven, Sir," the passerby says and raises his hat. The policemen agree that they should report to the police station by eight.

Right now we can see them approaching the market stalls. This is the time of day when business is most brisk. We can hear cackling chickens and the raised voices of vendors. Farther, in the back of the place where poultry is sold, in a small patch between the furrier's stall and the tailor's, clay pots are displayed for sale. Some have a brown shiny glaze, but most have their natural color. The policemen pass the vendors of poultry and of clay pots. A Gypsy woman, who had been telling two women their fortunes, is now dragging a little boy who clutches her skirt. Suddenly she disappears from our view. The policemen don't see her either. They look at and taste the fruit that they take out of the vendors' baskets. For a moment they hesitate. Then they buy a bag of sour cherries.

Hungry pigeons sneak among the laid-out goods. They peck at scattered lentils and linseed. They are audacious and dauntless.

The attorney sighs deeply. For a moment he feels a freezing chill on his lips as if the needles of mentholated hoarfrost settled on his tongue, lips, and palate. Mentholated hoarfrost, so much like the one many years ago, back in—it's incredible—but why count the years? Attorney Danilowski thinks again about Rosenzweig's tavern when he was twelve, or thirteen, or maybe fourteen years old. In the mouth of the boy who has been sucking mints the green mentholated needles turn into green interwoven with white as if in a watercolor. It was freezing cold when they were on their way to town. They could hear trees cracking. The frail cherry trees behind Rosenzweig's tavern were covered with frost, white, glassy, and crunchy if pressed. A strong eastern wind was blowing; it was Christmas Eve for the Eastern Orthodox, and the faithful were going to church. The two black horses shifted their weight, poked their noses in the snow, stomped, neighed, snorted out drops of spittle that instantly froze into crystals. On their nostrils, necks, and backs, white foam froze—Grandfather forgot to cover the horses with a blanket. Walek didn't go to the tavern, but with other boys romped around it. Yelling, they slid on the ground and threw snow at one another. Walek gave them mints that his grandfather had bought at the tavern. He had bought Walek a bag of anise drops as well but gave them to him on the way home. The boys chewed the mints or sucked them greedily and quickly so that they would get more, as if they were tasting such candy for the first time. Soon mentholated needles appeared around the mouth and on the fuzz which had already sprouted above the upper lip. They licked them and wiped them with their sleeves—the mentholated needles, light green interwoven with white, like frost on the boughs of the cherry trees, like leaves painted by frost on the windowpane and scraped off with a fingernail.

A white, thick, impenetrable layer of frost covered the tavern windows and the windows of the houses that stood behind the tavern on both sides of Gminna Street. Walek and the boys tried to peek inside, blowing on the windowpane or scratching the tangled-up, icy web. Then they blew on their reddened hands—which, it seemed, were about to freeze to the windowpane—put them under their sheepskin coats, and if that didn't help, into their mouths.

The snow lay high, reaching the knees, unbeaten except for a net of paths left by the pedestrians' shoes. It was hard and sharp; an icy crust had formed on its surface, which crunched at every step. The boys avoided the paths, looking for the places where they could plunge into the snow up to the waist, grab huge icy chunks, and throw them at one another, not aiming, blindly counting on luck. The dry and rustling snow sprinkled their coats and dropped inside their shirts where it melted and flowed down their warmed-up backs. Even the gloves and the boots were wet inside.

The horses, freed from the shaft, dipped their heads into the hay which the grandfather had loaded into the sleigh. Their bells jingled and sounded like the snow when the boys' feet crushed it. The boys' voices floated like soap bubbles, bounced off one another and wandered in every direction. The sharp jingle of the bells, sharp as the needles of frost glowing on the windowpane, rolled over the footpaths, roofs, and roads like ice balls the boys threw at pedestrians' feet.

"More! More!" shouted Walek when one of the boys fell down on his back. The others quickly covered him with snow—a huge snowdrift rose above him at once. They kept tearing off more white slabs, throwing them or laying them down if they were too heavy to throw. When their caps fell off, they stomped them into the snow, then shook them and put them back on, waiting for the lumps of snow to melt and trickle icily down their backs. The wind blew at their hair, threw snow in their eyes, flushed their faces.

Entering the tavern, Walek stumbled on a straw doormat and the whole place spun before his eyes. The doormat was frayed and creased, soaked with melted snow. The sour smell of fermenting wine, of beer tapped from the barrels, of vodka, and the nauseating smell of warmed-up bodies, sheepskin coats, leftover food—all those smells placed Walek in the world which he had watched through the little hole scratched in the windowpane. It was a world that he couldn't quite imagine.

Grandfather ordered a plate of sauerkraut stew ("Make sure the *bigos* is hot"). When Walek swallowed a few heaping spoonfuls, he felt his blood quicken in his feet and hands, and he wiped sweat drops off his forehead. The chunks of venison in the stew tasted different—did they?—from the venison and *bigos* cooked by his old aunt, Jadwiga, who was in charge of the Danilowskis' kitchen. And he, Walek, will never forget—because there are things, events, people that must never be forgotten—the taste of *bigos* eaten with rye bread, the meat carelessly chewed, the quickly cleaned plate. And he won't forget—because this mustn't be forgotten either—the taste of the first beer that he drank sitting in his grandfather's lap. Encouraged by the laughter of the amused patrons, Walek got away with his audacity because Grandfather pretended not to see what Walek was doing. After a few days when Grandfather told Walek's mother about it, she was shocked. In the name of God and in the name of Walek's love for her, she begged her son never to drink beer if he didn't want to see her dead. Walek promised he would never touch beer without her knowledge and permission.

A large spotted dog came out from under the table, raised its head, and started licking Walek's fingers. Behind the window, dusk was thickening, and the boys with whom Walek played could no longer be heard. Some patrons were going home, and others were taking their place. The faint light of kerosene lamps threw shadows on the walls. The smell of kerosene was spreading fast—faster than the darkness outside. The shadow of Rosenzweig, like the wings of a huge vulture, moved behind the counter, one time striking Walek with terror, another provoking him to mirth.

Attorney Danilowski has sucked the second mint on his way between Saint Augustine's Church and Orla Street. Evidently the time it takes to suck one mint is enough to pass the sacristy, Wendler's paint warehouse, Bat's shoe store, and then stop opposite Orla. If the attorney had put a third mint into his mouth and then a fourth one, he would have found himself on the stairs to his office. But maybe he has had enough sweets? Maybe so. The attorney stops in front of a barber shop and looks at his reflection in the window. He pulls up his collar and walks on.

Let us stop and look at the sky. In this account, intended as a detailed record of all events we witness, a chronicle of the events in the Book of the Day, we must not miss anything, not even the clouds. They too are preserved by our memory.

Describe the clouds? There are no clouds. There's no wind and there are no clouds. What can we see by staring persistently at the sky? A noisy flock of starlings flying from one cherry tree to another. If we are lucky, we may spot a hawk circling over the city.

Not even the slightest breeze moves the air. That doesn't mean, however, that the air is still. Quite the contrary. Honey-scented particles vibrate in the air, reminding us that the time of blooming and pollinating isn't over yet. In the diminutive gardens planted under the windows, the buzzing of bees alternately rises and falls. Life goes on.

Mrs. Zelda Baum walks out the door of her house, hesitates for a moment, not knowing whether to choose a shady or a sunny spot, and sits down on a bench in the sun. Insect wings flicker over the warm roof of the brewery. Mrs. Baum intently listens to their buzzing and watches the clouds of white, sour-smelling steam sliding down the brewery roof. She rolls up the sleeves of her dress and rests her palms on the edges of the bench. She closes her eyes. Nothing is happening.

Nothing is happening here—at the corner of Listopadowa and Lwowska. No smoke comes out of the pipe from the Baums' furnace. The cry of a hawk pierces the air; the third mint hasn't been put into the mouth; the steam slides down the roof.

Our statement that nothing is happening could be easily questioned by other observers. Let's add some new facts. Pigeons stroll on the roof of the Baums' shed. Mrs. Zelda Baum brushes the hair away from her forehead. Her eldest child spits out a piece of maggoty apple.

The grass near the brewery is wet, as if covered with dew. We're walking along the wall of the brewery down Listopadowa, leaving our footprints in the grass. The ashes from the Baums' furnace are gone. Soon our footprints will be gone.

Let's stop while they are still visible. Future events will negate them.

The policemen, Mr. Antoni Wrzosek and Mr. Tomasz Romanowicz, have decided to arrive at the police station late. They have no idea how to spend this free time, but thinking about it seems unnecessary. They have just left the market square, which is too noisy now. They're looking for a more secluded spot. They eat sour cherries, spitting the pits as far as they can. The pits land in the grass. It's not clear which of the men is the more accomplished spitter. The branches of walnut trees hang over their heads. Their heads get caught in the branches. The policemen breathe in the aromatic smell that resembles Eastern spices. Soon it'll be time to pick the green and still-soft fruit, cut it in half and pour, let's say, home brew over it. Will that do? The policemen don't know much about making walnut liqueur.

Their presence on Ogrodowa is accidental; it can't be explained in any other way. They could, for example, sit comfortably on the bridge across the Labunka and watch the outline of small, rapid waves and whirlpools, disappearing and always coming back in the same shape. An occupation as thrilling as eating sour cherries and smelling the walnuts.

We can't rule it out that Tomasz Romanowicz could keep Kazimiera M company. Better than anyone else, she knows the value of time. She has a reputation for conscientiousness and discretion. Hurried love appreciates such qualities. Romanowicz would enter the dark hallway. We would hear the floorboards squeak softly. A little light would come through the half-opened door to Kazimiera M's apartment. Right in front of her door Romanowicz would stumble on something. He would curse, placing his hand on the doorknob.

It could be this way. It could happen. Clothes and shoes would be scattered on the floor. Other items of the policeman's clothes would lie around in disarray: they might hang on the chair or across the bed rail. Maybe they couldn't be seen at all. In the sunbeam cutting through the curtain, we'd see Kazimiera M's pale body contrast with the policeman's beautifully tanned back. Chirping birds might be heard from behind the window.

On a warm day, with the body exposed to the sun, moving a hand can be an unpleasant necessity. Mrs. Zelda Baum knows it, and that's why she sits still and answers her daughter's questions with reluctance. She even tries not to hear them. She enjoys the quiet on Listopadowa and the sun that permeates her body. A moment of happiness as short as a breath.

Mr. Hershe Baum, standing behind the counter in his store, is certain that where he belongs—now, today—is here, behind the counter. He waits for his customers—many customers—because there's enough fabric for all. Mr. Baum would like to forget the store and his fussy customers for at least a month. But this is an infrequent and deeply hidden thought that Mr. Baum would never voice.

Attorney Danilowski is approaching his office. Black gravel grates under his feet. A sharp pebble has fallen into his shoe. The attorney bends down and removes the pebble gently. He looks at the tops of the linden trees, at the nests hanging there from which he can hear baby crows cawing. This seasonal cawing, which he hears in his office, doesn't irritate him. We may say that the attorney has already gotten used to those noisy concerts. His indifference to them means, no doubt, his acquiescence, his tacit assent, for which he expects nothing in return.

While the attorney is standing on the stairs to his office and turning the key in the lock, we realize that the position of the sun hasn't changed in the last few minutes. Presumably on Listopadowa the busy insect life continues, the steam still slides over the brewery roof, the bent-down grass on which we walked is straight again. We won't be mistaken if we say that Mrs. Zelda Baum is still sitting in front of the house, thinking about dinner while her daughter unsuccessfully demands answers to her childish, yet important questions, and Kazimiera M is taking a well-deserved nap.

The attorney has sat down in a soft chair and covered his face with his hands. He lightly massages his temples. He isn't really tired, he's only concerned about what soon awaits him. A series of boring cases about which he doesn't care, his clients' emotions which—thank God—he never shares. Confused plans and tedious duties.

(We should note a strange odor inside the office—a curious combination of the scent of flowers, paint, cigarette smoke, and of other, unfamiliar aromas, the source of which we can only guess. Since there are no flowers in the office, we wonder where the smell could be coming from. Could it be a lingering scent of perfume that smells like a bouquet of wild flowers? Blue cornflowers, whose presence in the bouquet is unmistakable, hint at the color of the sky, which their petals always reflect. There's a sweetly alluring smell of poppies that will reveal its full richness if we crush the petals into pulp. Also, a smell of chamomile, surrounded by the strong smell of yarrow. The smell of good-quality leather fills the office—such leather pads the door. Its smell resembles that of a shoe and leather goods store. The attorney dislikes this smell: it invariably reminds him of the skinning and disemboweling of roe deer shot by his grandfather and father. He once watched that with an interest which he now finds disturbing and difficult to explain. The association may seem farfetched and puzzling to outsiders, yet it is relevant for the attorney. It comes to mind every morning as he walks through the door of his office.)

Sitting behind his desk, the attorney looks over today's newspapers. He notices an item on the burning of a flour mill in

Jozefow. In fact, he remembers having heard about it recently. He isn't interested in agricultural news, containing the forecasts about this year's crops. The forecasts, he thinks, smack of sophistry. They are ludicrous. He sees an item about a group of Warsaw actors coming to stage a play that has had a lot of publicity in the capital. On the whole nothing is here that would radically alter the course of life in town. Nothing that would bewilder or agitate him. He succumbs to overpowering boredom.

Consequently, the attorney rolls the newspapers and puts them away into a drawer. He's left with an empty desk, a metal ashtray on top. Through the open window, he looks at the linden trees, at the light flickering among the leaves. Sitting like that or standing near the window, he could watch the trees for hours, he could listen to the cawing crows and the various sounds that come from the street—he could identify and interpret each noise.

He thinks about the theater, taps a tune on the desk. He no longer remembers when and where he heard the tune the first time. Maybe Warsaw? He can't tell. How did he pick it up? How among the shreds of past events can he find the moment in which this tune turned into something more permanent? Could it now exist apart from his recollections?

A ringdove has flown by the window, its wing flashing metallically. The time is 9:27.

The attorney stops tapping the tune. He takes out his papers, looks at the correspondence. He wants to review the case that he's studied so many times before. The case concerns his client's—Mariusz Mroz's—ill-fated tenancy near Zwierzyniec. The case is like many others, nothing new for the attorney, but the entanglements it presents are disproportionate to its importance, and it keeps changing in light of his client's words. Attorney Danilowski reads on the second page: ". . . then, after his death, together with the land on which it stands, inherited by my nephew . . ." And a few lines below: ". . . so the well I'm thinking about, according to what you know, Sir . . ." The attorney skips a few lines of the letter. His eyes stop on the last words of the same page: ". . . she kindly agreed to keep an eye on the well that is visible from her house . . ." Here the attorney finishes reading the letter. He folds the sheets filled out with meticulous handwriting and slides them into an envelope.

A bee has flown into the office. Buzzing loudly—perhaps it's loaded with too much pollen—it is flying like a bird locked up in a cage. It wants to get out of the unexpected trap like a siskin caught in an alder grove in winter. When the bee comes near the attorney's head, he waves it away with an envelope that contains Mr. Mroz's letter. (Maybe the bee is attracted to the smell of the mint drop that the attorney was eating.) The bee lands on a corner of the desk—the envelope can't reach it there. Then it flies off and, spiraling, heads for the wall opposite the window. It tries to hold on to the rough surface. When that fails, the bee lights on a cabinet. Raising its abdomen, it walks back and forth, and then once again attempts to storm the wall.

The attorney recalls that as a child he caught bees on flowers. Gently, yet quickly, you had to seize the bee's wings with two fingers. And since your right hand was occupied, you had to use the fingers of your left hand to remove the pollen attached to the bee's hind legs, near the abdomen. The pollen was sweet and tasty, and the bee, set free, continued to busy itself with flowers.

But this bee won't find rest among sweet and soft petals. It is flying straight for the large mirror opposite the attorney's desk. A few reconnaissance rounds and the bee hits the mirror with all its strength, convinced that the mirror is the open space behind the window.

(Pulling the legs off one by one and finally the wings, you

could watch the jerky movements of the abdomen and the bulging eyes which knew and saw everything—they seemed to Walek unusually bulging. He would put each leg in turn into his mouth, and having sucked enough pollen, he would spit out the legs and throw away the bee's body.)

The office is calm. The attorney doesn't move. He doesn't want to scare the bee. The bee still believes the mirror promises freedom. The bee comes close to the glass and tries to cross to the other side. It slides down, frantically beating its wings.

(After pulling off the bee's legs and wings, you could stick a thin and stiff blade of grass into the bee's mouth and slowly push the blade of grass down. Manipulating the blade carefully, Walek saw its end come out the abdomen. Together with a small drop of liquid, the stinger—which was the reason for this operation—slid out. Sometimes Walek would end up getting stung. It was his sacrifice for a fascinating adventure.)

The bee, tired from the endless attempts to get to the other side of the mirror, falls to the floor. It buzzes quietly. The bee's legs and wings keep moving. The bee starts walking towards the window, one meter above the floor. It makes its last effort to fly to the linden trees visible from where it is now, but it doesn't reach the window—it lands in the middle of the desk. Motionless, the bee stays there a short time. Then it heads for the ashtray. The attorney swats the bee with the envelope, and in an instant we see the insect turn over, its legs up, moving frantically. The attorney unscrews the top of the fountain pen and plunges the stylus in where the bee's abdomen begins. The tip of the stylus meets the resistance of the table. The bee is hanging in the air. The attorney carefully examines the insect. There's some pollen left on its legs. He pulls off one wing, then the other. One by one he pulls off the legs. He can see that the bee is still alive. Its eyes twitch. With a fingernail he nudges the bee's body into the ashtray, then the abdomen, wings, legs. He squashes the bee's head with the blunt end of the fountain pen.

This quite unexciting incident seems to bode well for the rest of the day. No matter what else happens today, the attorney doesn't consider his early morning wasted.

"So what do you advise me about the well, Sir?" Mariusz Mroz, sitting before the attorney, fixes his eyes on the ashtray.

"Until the case is clarified, I'd insist on locking the well. I believe that a sturdy cover, a latch, a padlock . . ."

"I've thought of that. But even in the most sturdy cover there will be cracks through which someone may throw . . ."

"I understand. And in fact I don't know what answer to give you."

Mr. Mariusz Mroz looks at the attorney without a trace of relief. After a while he directs his eyes at the ashtray. The attorney takes a sheet of paper out of a drawer, tears the paper into pieces, and throws them on the remains of the insect.

"How is your grain crop?" In the attorney's question there is only a distant echo of curiosity.

"Thank you. It was unexpectedly good. The wheat looks fine, the oat hasn't quite grown. I expect a good harvest of plums. Over by the meadows, where the trees are exposed, some flowers froze in the spring. Those that survived set beautiful fruit, amazingly firm and full."

Mariusz Mroz goes on talking. He says something about bees and about the abundance of blooming flowers on the unmown meadows, about the honey smell of the forest and of the orchards. The attorney listens, yet doesn't hear. He is in and is not in the office. He keeps falling into an indescribable softness.

Rainstorms that raged for more than a week over the region left puddles, microscopic swamps in which water was distilled through leaves and time. Among larger clumps of grass—

cocksfoot, timothy, rye. Among clusters of white clover, yarrow. In the holes left by horses' hooves.

One must look at the water carefully. It's light green, perhaps a little blue. Walek dips his fingers in it and raises them to his nose. The water smells of rotting roots, of soil black as soot and clammy. He stirs the bottom with his finger. In a little puddle float parts of roots, seed husks, and a beetle's chitin.

Everything spins for a moment, rises to the surface, sinks, rises one more time. Walek can hear his own breath. Squatting, his head squeezed between his knees, he hears his heart beating. The water becomes transparent again. A ray of light bounces off the delicately rippled surface, pierces it, refracts, and rests at the bottom. As if in a mirror, an image of a dragonfly shows in the water.

Walek takes one step and the water spurts out—black drops run down his thighs. Lifting his leg—he lifts it slowly as if waiting for something—he hears the mud make a low smacking sound, escaping, it seems, from some untold depths, from some mysterious source. Maybe it is a sigh of creatures living under the surface. The leg is suspended in the air. He has to listen to what will happen next. The black hole the size of his foot has quickly filled with water, still moving, as if uncertain whether it will have to give in to the pressure again. What is there to hear? Leaves rustling overhead, a bubble of air rising from the bottom. The damned souls, the damned souls of moles, otters, hares don't make a sound. Walek holds his breath. Another dragonfly (maybe it's the same one) flies over him; its wings, with a net of dark veins, sparkle and whir. It flies lower and lands on the top of a thistle. Maybe he'll catch it. He won't. A few centimeters away from the dragonfly, the hand stops, embarrassed. The dragonfly has flown away, half real, like a moving shadow.

One step forward, two, three. The legs up to the knees are

smeared with mud, which dries instantly and leaves a grey coat. Walek is looking for a deeper hole and slowly inserts one leg, then the other. His pants, pulled up high, pinch. There's a ditch nearby and a small bridge across it. Walek walks there, and standing on the bridge, takes off his pants and hangs them on the rickety railing.

Here life is irrepressible, blind, wild. The water evaporates rapidly, carrying away the swampy odor of rotting leaves, blooming flowers, grass, and fish slime. Patiently, Walek waits for something. What he's waiting for may happen any second now. He can sense it. But he must be able to see and to hear. He sits down on the edge of the ditch close to the bridge. He drops his legs into the water. All that's supposed to happen, all that he's waiting for, is already here now. The water is warm, yet somehow it relaxes, its coolness wandering from the feet up to the hands and the back.

Water-thyme entwines his fingers. Tiny snails hidden in thin shells are entangled in it. The shells are most often black, rarely light. Sometimes there may be one that's yellow or mixed—striped or streaked. Water-thyme must be handled gently because it's tangled up. Walek separates the plants from one another. A shell with a snail inside falls out, still slimy but quickly drying. The snail walks slowly on Walek's palm, exploring the unknown territory. It may be thrown into the water. A barely audible splash and the revolving shell settles on the muddy bottom. The shell may settle with its opening up. If the opening is down, it may be possible to see the snail move on the slime or rest on an underwater leaf.

There, among the leaves, a silver globe glistens. It's an air bubble. Walek wants to look at it. Carefully, he steps into the ditch. He feels coolness, even though the water is warm. He puts his hands under the water, picks up the gossamer bubble, squeezes it, and the air escapes above the surface. It can't be seen. It's gone.

The light breeze breaks up into many different layers of smell. There's a smell of soggy, swollen earth, a smell of sow-thistle, of marsh-marigolds, long out of bloom (maybe the smell of marigolds isn't really there, maybe it's only Walek's guess), and a smell of fish that have been thrown out of the water. The smells are intense and, as each year, enticing.

But a little farther up the river where spring flood water doesn't dry, towards willow brake and nettles, you can make your way through the reeds and gather armfuls of waist-high brown reed-mace. From there Walek can hear a hoarse sound. Is a horsefly buzzing? A frog croaking? The meadow whispers, sings, groans more and more persistently. Walek listens, enraptured. He tries to make out each voice of this meadow chorus: the wailing of a wild duck, the rustling of grass. Premonitions. Suppositions. Nothing else.

One more time Walek bends down and rakes the grass with his fingers. The huge garden of nettles, thistles, reeds becomes a disturbingly small reflection. Walek must look more carefully, more keenly. He squats as he did when he stirred water with his finger. Now, descending to the sources, to the root (it's not a metaphor), probing with curious fingers, penetrating with even more curious eyes, he can see where—as an old Gypsy woman says—the line of life runs and how long it is. He can see where the line of life will cross the line of death. So this is an important place.

"Are you listening, Sir?"

"Yes, of course, I'm listening."

So Walek is at the source. Here he can see everything that was only a false conjecture. The lifeline originates between the forefinger and the thumb. It ends—not always—in the wrist. It may be deep, straight, clear. It may be different. Everybody knows those short, shallow, somewhat hesitant lines. What do they bode? A person's life, of which the line is a sign, will give the best answer.

Digging his heels in the peat, Walek grasps the stalk and pulls it up. A quiet, barely audible hiss. It gives a certain idea, allows an insight into the physiology of grass. The meadow is in bloom—still in bloom. In the tall grass, behind the reeds, Walek can't be seen. He relishes such moments.

Where it starts, Walek's lifeline is crisscrossed with tiny stripes. (All the truths and untruths, all the dreams and awakenings of his earliest years should be counted. They alone formed the beginning of the lifeline.) Nearer the wrist, the line is slightly circular, distinct, unbroken. What does that bode? And this isn't everything. Somewhere in the second half of the line he can see a delicately cut line that runs diagonally down. The line is short, and Walek can't find where it ends. He feels helpless. What can it all mean? Fascinating speculations.

When he looks up—for a very short time, a few seconds—it seems to him that he is a reed or a willow twig, or a thistle, its purple flowers looted by bumblebees. In those few seconds he can be a dark blue or reddish brown dragonfly, or a stray bee loaded with pollen.

Where he's squatting now, there are more snails than in the ditch or in the river. Although these are bigger, they look very much like the other ones, hidden in their fragile shells. But there is also a different kind of snail with no shell, thin and oblong. Have they left their shells? Walek doesn't know. He slides a stalk under a snail that's gliding on a sow-thistle. The snail curls up, hides its horns, and almost at once encircles the stalk and straightens its horns.

The lines in the palms of Walek's sister resemble his own. If you look carefully, you'll see that his sister's lines are actually like his father's. The father's palms are the prototypes of Walek's. If it weren't for the inevitable changes wrought by time in Pawel Danilowski's palms, Walek's hands would be exact replicas of his father's. His father's hands show the marks of many cuts, and their skin, though still delicate and white, has lost its former firmness. But let's go back to the lifeline. On Mr. Pawel Danilowski's left hand—Walek has checked it often—a small line branches off in the middle of the lifeline. It's worth noting this offshoot is clearer in his father's palm, and, as in Walek's, its end gets lost among other lines. Apparently, Pawel Danilowski has no idea about it. He has never looked at his hands with much attention.

Walek breaks the stalk of a reed. Some of these stalks are bored by worms—white, short, active. Around them, as in a maggoty plum or apple, there are a lot of brown lumps. This is chewed, digested reed. With the help of a sharp leaf, Walek removes the worm from its leaf and puts it on his hand. The worm turns over, shrinks, straightens. It tries to go somewhere—but where? It moves towards Walek's fingers. Walek throws it in the water. The worm sinks down, turns over, curls up, starts going somewhere. (It's no good if the lifeline is short and stops abruptly at the base of the thumb.) Perhaps tomorrow, when Walek comes here—he'll come for sure—when he looks at the water, the worm will lie stretched out or strangely curled up, still, swollen, as if blown up. In a few days—Walek doesn't know if he'll be here in a few days and if he'll find this spot—the worm will be floating on the surface. But this isn't certain either. In a few days, if the weather is fine and if it's warm, like today, the water in those tiny swamps will dry and disappear with no trace. The worm will change color, turn brown, and its body will disintegrate into unidentifiable pieces.

When you are at the source, it's useful to examine other stalks as well, to split them with a fingernail. Everything inside them is interesting. Walek knows the importance of his meticulous investigation. It's warm, very warm. Dandelions are blooming, so many of them that in some places the meadow is yellow, not green. Sweat trickles down Walek's back. The evaporating water forms drops on his legs and back. He rises slowly. His legs are numb. He starts walking to the river. Here the water is unexpectedly cold, its current swift. He can see the yellow, thick-grained sand. Sticklebacks and roaches flash by. Walek is standing in the water—the swan mussel shells and big shells of snails glisten. He takes water into his hands, pours it over his back. Dragonflies buzz, one, two, three. The water doesn't reach his waist. He squats, submerges.

". . . so the bees didn't benefit from clover. Buckwheat looks good. If you went into a buckwheat field, you'd hear constant buzzing. As usual, it's a beautiful time now where we live, in Zwierzyniec. Forest, good air, quiet."

"Would you like a mint drop?"

In front of the building, in the linden trees, it's quiet. We are standing in the shade. There's shade on the pavement, only here and there a sunny patch, and a few sun rays that managed to break through the leaves.

Outside the attorney's office window we can hear a subdued conversation. The attorney's and his client's words mingle with the sounds of the town: someone laughs, cab horses snort, a cranky child cries. Noon is approaching. Hot air flows from green-and-red roof tiles, and from copper-colored roofs, down the walls beneath the open windows, onto the street under the pedestrians' feet.

We should take another photograph—wait, not yet! Standing under the linden trees, let's try to capture the moment when the heat billowing over the roofs will start to radiate its own light, a kind of luminosity known to those who have watched a bonfire or clouds. Before a thunderstorm, clouds glow with an unusual internal light which enlivens them with luminous colors and their various halftones: yellow, pink, blue, green, purple. Watching the air over a bonfire is like watching clouds that promise a thunderstorm, that are a few breaths away from the first drop of rain.

Rosenzweig's tavern is full. The door, pushed by entering patrons, swings like a pendulum. Although the windows are open, the tavern is filled with smoke. In the tavern everyone smokes what he has—cigars, sometimes a pipe, or hand-rolled cigarettes. Rosenzweig isn't smoking. He doesn't have time, at least not now. He fills beer steins until they overflow, then he stands them on the counter. They disappear quickly. The moment a patron picks up a stein, Rosenzweig deftly wipes the countertop with a damp and dirty rag. It's a practiced gesture, repeated countless times. On the top of the counter, threads of water and beer can be seen, their shape determined by the sweep of the rag. But soon, almost immediately—perhaps right at the moment when the tavern owner lifts the rag up—the threads of beer and water are no longer threads. They change into evenly spaced drops. Before we get a chance to look at them, Rosenzweig places the overflowing steins on the counter and destroys the finely wrought landscape of fragile threads and drops. As if to annihilate and eradicate from memory the landscape of threads and drops. (We remember: Rainstorms that raged for more than a week over the region left puddles, microscopic swamps in which water was distilled through leaves and time. Among larger clumps of grass—cocksfoot, timothy, rye. Among clusters of white clover, yarrow. In the holes left by horses' hooves.) Like the flood that drowns the town or destroys the harmony of the spring meadow . . . the drought that dries out tiny meadow swamps . . . the fire that burns everything. *Go back a few steps and turn your face away.*

Rosenzweig looks up from the beer steins. Bent over the wet counter, his hands resting on it, he stares through the open window at the marketplace, perhaps trying to recognize someone's distant silhouette.

Rosenzweig is also a pigeon breeder. Persian butterflies—doesn't it sound beautiful? He installed his pigeon coop in the garret above the tavern. The birds leave through an opening in the southern side of the roof. On a summer afternoon, when the tin roof heats up, they perch on the ladders attached to the top of the roof. Up there, where the pigeons get into the coop, the commotion is the same as in the tavern—not all the pigeons are flying. We'd have to strain our eyes to see their wings flash high over tavern and town.

Every now and then Rosenzweig leaves his place behind the counter, steps outside and watches the pigeons. He must know which ones are flying, how long they've been flying, and how well. Rosenzweig is a great expert on pigeons and he can judge the flying style of his birds. He is standing in the sun, shading his eyes, and looking up. He sees, or maybe he only thinks he does, the birds' wings flash. The pigeons have been over the town for five hours already—how much longer will they fly today?

One more time he raises his hand to his forehead, squats, looks up. He picks up a pebble and throws it at the pigeons. All of them rise. First chaotically, then as a compact flock, they climb higher and higher. Rosenzweig watches them a while longer and then returns to his counter.

The sun has risen higher. The clock hand on the Town Hall has moved. Rosenzweig's pigeons beat their wings rhythmically, trace wider and wider circles, and reflect the light.

Two women leave Mr. Baum's fabric store, carrying folded pieces of fabric. Mr. Hershe Baum is at the store alone. It's empty and quiet here if one forgets the noise made by the pigeons. He lifts the countertop and walks toward the door. Behind the window, the vines move, swung by leaping pigeons.

He stops in the doorway—for a moment the chirping subsides—and looks at the marketplace. He takes an olive green apple from his pocket and bites it. He returns someone's greetings, takes another bite.

If the door weren't open, the store would be dusky. And it would be hot. The half-opened windows and the wide-opened door create a draft that causes the vine leaves to sway in the space between the window and the frame.

Standing in the door to his store, the merchant observes the sky with great interest. He looks at Rosenzweig's pigeons, which leisurely yet systematically soar, joining those pigeons that have been flying since morning. With a practiced eye Mr. Hershe Baum watches their fluent, faultless flight. His pigeons too fly beautifully. Today, as always, they are flying. We had a chance to see them this morning when he was clapping his hands to spur them on. From here Mr. Hershe Baum can't see his pigeons—they are too far away.

The smell of freshly brewed coffee—the time is 10:40—wafts through Kazimiera M's apartment. Kazimiera M has pulled the curtains apart and opened the window. She can be seen dawdling about her room. She stops in front of the mirror, comes closer, very close to it, and examines—how to say it more precisely?—her naked body. Her right nipple rubs the mirror. Its coolness, like the coolness of an early morning, at once spreads all over her body. In Kazimiera M's eyes we can detect intense self-adoration, the kind of curiosity that we sometimes exhibit when observing someone else's nakedness.

Kazimiera M slips on a dressing gown, but she doesn't button it up. Its flaps brush against her hips and legs. She returns to the mirror, flounces her hair. She places both hands under her breasts, squeezes them, and thrusts them forward. It seems that the skin around the nipples is wrinkled. That's where Kazimiera M's attention is focused. With her two forefingers she massages the nipples in circles. After a while this action brings the awaited result. The barely visible defect—the result of her clients' and friends' amorous desires—disappears without a trace. Something else happens as well. The nipples grow erect, taut as if under the pressure of milk. They remind Kazimiera M of the way they look after Romanowicz nibbles them. She smiles discreetly at the memory of those adventures. She wets her lips in a cup, takes a small swallow of hot coffee. A few small black hairs have stood up on her breasts. Kazimiera M doesn't know what a precious addition and adornment those hairs are. None of her clients or friends has ever mentioned them to her.

She sits down opposite the window. The sun comes into the room unobstructed. Her dressing gown is now buttoned from the waist down. Above it, the gown opens, showing her breasts. The light streams over her pale skin. It sparkles in her long hair, inlaying it with glittering gems. Half a cup of coffee is still left. She drinks it, snacking on a sweet pastry.

The leaves of a pear tree shading the Baums' house are slowly losing their freshness, but they haven't shriveled yet. All of them shine. It's getting hotter and stuffier. In front of the house, hens scratch the ground. Someone shouts behind the brewery gate.

Kazimiera M lifts the cup to her lips. She feels relaxed and rested. Close by she places a small oval mirror, a token of the attorney's affection and memory. The mirror, framed in light polished wood, is decorated with carved plant ornaments: exotic leaves, flowers, fruit. She picks the mirror up, brings it to her face, looks at it closely. She presses her lips together or pouts, and with her fingers examines the skin on her cheek. She brushes the hair away from her forehead.

Right in front of the window, clouds of small flies float in the air. They float like weightless objects. It's impossible to predict where they will fly. One of them may stray into the room. Sometimes they fly in swarms, like mosquitoes on a warm afternoon.

A wild pigeon flaps its wings and settles on a branch of the pear tree, but we can't see it. Muffled, uninterrupted cooing is now coming from the direction of the tree.

Kazimiera M puts the mirror away. She moistens her fore-finger in perfume and dabs it on the skin near her ears. The last swallow of coffee is decidedly less tasty than the ones before. Tiny bits of coffee grounds, which she can't spit out, have remained in her mouth. With her fingers she removes them from her teeth and the tip of her tongue. The taste of coffee blends with the sweetly sour taste of perfume. Her lips stretch in a mild grimace. Unhurriedly, she starts to comb her hair. She bends her head sideways, then backwards. She squints. She looks at the mirror, then straight ahead, out the window.

The disk of the sun has caught onto the top of the pear tree. For a moment, motionless, it tarries there.

It seems that pieces of the sun disk, like shards of a shattered stained-glass window, slide down the leaves and the branches. The light in the grass, under and around the pear tree, is most likely a fragment of a shattered stained-glass disk. Thanks to it, we sight a bundle of grey feathers: a wild pigeon perching between the forking branches.

Another wagon is going to the flour mill. It passes Kazimiera M's house. Several meters farther it turns left. It has arrived at its destination.

The Baums' children have come to play under Kazimiera M's window. With a thick stick they draw lines, circles, and figures on the path. Where the drawings end they stick leafy lilac twigs. Only the children understand what purpose these twigs serve. They talk, laugh, walk over the drawings, following the route no one else knows.

In the meantime the pigeon has left the pear tree. It is flying over the brewery. It disappears.

It can be seen one more time.

It's gone again.

The white steam no longer slides from the roof. The grass around the brewery is completely dry. We can lie down on it and, pressing the ear to the ground, hear (or rather intuit, guess: after all, either intuition or guesswork will be reliable) the grass pulsate with the quick rhythm of life—the sound of flowing sap, the murmur of a wandering ant.

Kazimiera M has finished grooming. We can see her before a mirror buttoning her dress. The dress is green with large white flowers on it. Using a horn clasp, she fastens her hair in the back. Barefooted, she stands on her toes, she raises her hands, joins them over her head, stretches and turns around. The scent of perfume permeates Kazimiera M's room. It seems she has used the most becoming kind. She bends down and puts on her shoes.

The crowing of a rooster drowns the noise made by the frolicking children. The crowing issues from the bottom of its gut; it is remarkably drawn out and resonant, as if it were the last signal before something that we are unable to foresee. The time is 11:10. Maybe it's the annunciation of the noon?

Several wagons wait in front of the flour mill. A goat and some hens jostle among them. Two women are returning from the market square. In the brewery the machines drone incessantly. Mrs. Zelda Baum is carrying logs from the shed to the apartment. In the schoolyard on Lwowska Street children shout and shriek.

Once again the crowing of a rooster tears the air. Kazimiera M leaves her apartment. She takes a footpath to Spadek—that's the closest way to the market square. However, we don't really know where she is walking. Upon seeing her, for no apparent reason the children run away, tripping and breaking the lilac twigs.

The Baums' apartment is grey from smoke. Mrs. Zelda Baum is airing it: she has opened the door and all the windows. This is nothing new. It's the smoke from the straw that she has used to light the wood in the cast-iron stove. She rubs her teary eyes and coughs. In no time the fire will start howling in the stove, slipping yellow and red tongues of flame through the stove lids and cracks.

Another wagon can be seen on Listopadowa. The horses' hooves rhythmically beat the cobblestones. The wagon is heading toward Lwowska. It is carrying flour. The driver half-heartedly swings the whip, takes a drag on a cigarette. We are watching where he will turn. He enters Lwowska and turns in the direction of Kalinowice. Someone jumps onto the wagon, shakes the driver's hand, sits down on a sack.

Pigeons walk on the ground in front of the Baums' house. They are looking for millet and rapeseeds. Or maybe for small pebbles. Through the window Mrs. Zelda Baum tosses a handful of groat offal that her husband bought.

The children have come back under Kazimiera M's window. They have brought newly picked lilac twigs, a few sticks, flat and round stones with which they are building some kind of edifice. Maybe it's a palace surrounded by beautiful gardens. They decorate the palace with pieces of broken glass. Are they stained-glass windows? We don't know.

Sweat glistens on Rosenzweig's face. It flows down his neck, behind his unbuttoned vest. The air in the tavern is warm and humid. Airing won't help. Who knows, maybe the heat comes in together with the noise from the market square. Rosenzweig takes off his yarmulke and scratches his head. The clients ask for slivovitz. Rosenzweig hands them the liquor, twisting his grey sidecurl on his forefinger. This day will surely never end.

We must wait before we take more pictures. The leaves of the pear tree are already quite limp, but this isn't the moment we are waiting for. This isn't the moment when the pupil of the cat's eye exposed to the sun will be the narrowest—when it will be a thin line.

"This day will surely never end!" Rosenzweig pours vodka. The patrons, a bit groggy, in unbuttoned shirts, follow up the liquor with a bite of herring or sausage. They smoke tobacco, joke loudly, and tell stories about the most interesting events of the last few days. Those events are true and familiar to everyone; they are somewhat disturbing, and like any recent news they are interesting as well as instructive. Every opportunity that can bring experience should be used. Rosenzweig listens attentively to the stories. From the sphere of probability, he throws in details and facts known only to him. He is—as he should be—reserved when he informs everyone that this is a unique category of facts. The patrons rub their palms gleefully: "This is the news none of us has heard."

"Hush!" It's a secret known only to Rosenzweig. What could have happened is as important as what did happen. "So, dear Sirs, hush!"

By now we can see Rosenzweig holding a long fork. Out of a large glass jar, he takes herring with bulging eyes and frayed tails. The herring smell of salt, pepper, and bay leaf. And of wild mustard seed. In the jar, flaked off scales drift. They float on the surface of the marinade like duckweed. They are silver. Rosenzweig licks his finger, which drips marinade. He adjusts his yarmulke.

The first of Rosenzweig's pigeons is finishing a half-day of flying. Several wide circles over the market square, and the pigeon lands on top of the roof. Its wings are down. Other pigeons are still flying.

Above the benches, above the heads of Rosenzweig's patrons,

a picture painted on wood hangs on the wall. The tavern and the patrons are watched by a little town with sand-colored houses. The sun suspended over their roofs undoubtedly looks after the town, which is submerged in pleasant warmth. Over the town, among white clouds, people with spread arms soar. Something else soars too—we don't know what—but it's something colorful. The soaring people and the colorful objects are wrapped in flames. A fiery ball, followed by smoke and a tail of sparks, rolls on a narrow street. Some people standing in the market square look at the ball or at those who soar in the sky. Some of those standing in the middle of the town begin to rise from the ground on their way to the clouds. The scene is like a snapshot from an improbable dream. The picture has been hanging here for years, dusted many times, but it seems that no one has examined it carefully.

In front of Rosenzweig's tavern, horses are getting impatient. Still harnessed, they scuffle. They snort, neigh, try to bite their own necks. They have been standing here for years—always the same horses, yet every day they're different. Chestnut, bay, and grey. Someone walks among them, caressingly strokes their sides, and from each wagon takes out a handful of hay. As usual he does it unobserved, unseen by anyone.

The market square is emptying. Those who are most persistent stay. A droshky in front of Baum's store, a few wagons in front of Rosenzweig's tavern. The doors to the stores rarely open, and the stalls are deserted. In the shade a panting dog lies. The Gypsy woman roams the market square with her little son. The sun is motionless.

"Good Sir, pretty Sir, let the Gypsy tell your fortune."

Mr. Mariusz Mroz is leaving the attorney's office. He looks at his watch. He has talked too long to the attorney. He is walking in the direction of the Town Hall. The clock on the Town Hall shows the same hour as his watch.

Shadows spread on the attics. The streets are cool and breezy. Mr. Mariusz Mroz buys lemonade. The bells of Saint Thomas's Church have sounded. Mr. Mroz makes his way toward a restaurant near the Town Hall. He'd like to eat dinner. In front of the Town Hall two idle droshkys stand. The cab-drivers sit on the steps, talk, and smoke cigarettes. Mr. Mroz enters the restaurant. A lace curtain stirs on the glass door.

The swallows chirp endlessly over the town. On the lawns, flowers are aflame with fiery colors.

In the park, fish break the surface of the pond. The water is green and warm. The fish stick their mouths over the water level as if to get some air or catch an insect flying low. Or maybe they want—we can't hear anything—to shout something. And now the circles disperse slowly, one circle lapping over another. And so on. They disperse like an echo that bounces off the trees and the brake. The duckweed, in some places half a finger thick, effectively keeps the new circles from dispersing.

Swallows race over the pond, their flight fast and oblique. Will they pass the winter here? Flying, they brush the water, rinse their feathers.

The pond breathes. The park breathes. The sun rolls on the pond like a shiny ball. Its rays move across the water as if they were spokes in a moving wheel. The breath of the park surrounds us, engulfs us. We have to undo our buttons. We'll take a picture of this sun ball, which someone let loose on the water. It is still rolling as it was a second ago, the circles dispersing and the rays rushing over the surface, over the duckweed. The swallows surge in their flight. The sun rocks on the water. The ducks, flapping their wings, fly off the grass and land in the middle of the pond. The sun ball rises from the water.

Another photograph for our collection:

A blurred and fuzzy spot—how many times has it happened

already?—in the place of the beating wings. The ducks are flying away from the pond, their webbed feet skimming the water. The water ripples in a series of small circles until the leg touches the pond for the last time. One, two, three rounds over the park (this isn't in the photograph), and the ducks disappear behind the tops of the horse-chestnut trees.

Meanwhile the sun leaps. It bounces off the pond, approaches its point of permanent suspension, and again falls onto the water. The immobile kingdom of noon has become mobile. The sun and the clock on the Town Hall—almost identical, immobile sources of mobility. Even those objects that usually don't move, now move and undulate. Those two sources determine everything. Nothing takes place without their consent.

We are standing on a narrow bridge. Shading our eyes, we look ahead. On the opposite shore of the pond, beyond the islet, we can see a white spot—it's a swan.

The next photograph:

The dome of the Town Hall is the second sun. But it's a bit different from the first one, which unfortunately the photograph can't show. This second sun is somewhat greenish, having most likely bathed in the pond. Now there are two suns over the town, both equally large, both equally mobile and immobile. We already know that both beams are the source of light flashing on the surface of the pond. Farther, beyond the dome of the Town Hall, beyond the second sun, the sky is a little hazy, creating the illusion that our eyesight is imperfect. The tops of the horse-chestnut and linden trees, the tops of the churches crowned with crosses. Not a single bird. The town floats in light.

And one more photograph, this time from a different observation point:

Again, after many years, someone happens to look at the

picture which won't reveal the slightest traces of what we wanted to seize from time. It seems the moment has come when we should capture with the lens a fragment of a house, a fragment of a greenish roof, when we should try to preserve on a piece of photographic paper the image of hot air billowing over the tin roof. We release the shutter. This moment—already—has happened. The roof glows, the sky is empty above it. Blooming flowers in the open windows. Bright, shiny plaster with gashes. All around, swallows chirp.

The cabdrivers are sitting on the steps of the Town Hall. Mariusz Mroz is leaving the restaurant called Under the Sign of the Horn. The door slams, the curtain stirs. He walks toward a droshky. The horses are tired and hot. Their black hair glistens when lazily they turn in front of the Town Hall. The droshky passes the Salt Market and keeps going farther.

Some more commotion in the linden trees outside the attorney's office. The branches sway together with the nests. The attorney reviews the papers, makes corrections. He looks ahead, through the window. Nothing changes in the order of things.

Everything is the way it was. In the park the sun bounces off the pond and at the same time stands still. A fish's mouth sticks out of the water. Hot air whirls over the roofs. The town floats around the Town Hall. Everyone floats.

In the light of the Town Hall dome—the second sun—the dust under the feet of the pedestrians turns yellow. The dust rises from the cobblestones, together with the beams of light. Wheels, horses' hooves, and shoes stir it up.

The sun strikes the eyes like sharp snow. A cabdriver opens his mouth wide and yawns. His large mustache, black and handsome, arches delicately. He puts the bits into the horses' mouths and adjusts their collars. The horses toss their heads nervously and shake their manes. Passing his hand along the horse's side, he comes to the droshky. He leaves. The walls of the houses in the Salt Market amplify the echo of the wheels and hooves. From a distance, the horses' croups glisten.

Morando Street—the bridge for light. Let the pious Hasidim run in like light. Let them take their wide-brimmed hats in their hands. Raising them, let the Hasidim sing joyous songs that glorify the Highest. The tallithim reflect the light. Their coats stream. The words from the holy books will resound in the marketplace of the two suns. The holy Hasidim will hold hands and dance in a circle.

As we have expected, the pupil of the cat's eye is now a narrow slit. The cat pokes its head through the gate and, undaunted, looks carefully. It squints. Its eyes show the midday weariness and savagery of one that frequents garbage dumps and cellars. The street is empty, and the cat's eyes are fixed on us. The sun glides over its coat. The cat returns to the gate and disappears in the cool and the dark.

Meanwhile the merry dance of the Hasidim still continues in front of the Town Hall, and we want it to continue. The Hasidim approach the lawns, careful not to miss a step. The light of both suns frolics on the surfaces of flowers and leaves. The grass—let's bend our heads down to look from close by—is a living study of chiaroscuro. The white stockings of the Hasidim are covered with the rising dust. Their song sails over the town.

Our suppositions have come true. The leaves of the pear tree in front of the Baums' house are limp and dull. Their edges curl inward. The sun is still hooked to the top of the pear tree. Wasps and bees buzz.

A goat has come from near the flour mill. The animal munches apples. It's impossible to keep it from mischief. It wags its tail and moves its ears to keep the flies away.

Again the steam slides down the brewery roof and wall. It's warm and it smells of fermented yeast.

Everything begins and ends at this moment. A pigeon's grey flight reduces space, and suddenly Listopadowa is connected to Mlynska Street, against the established order that Lwowska imposes. The pigeon disappears in one of the orchards on Mlynska. Listopadowa is where it has been: on one side we have the brewery, on the other the Baums' house and shed, Kazimiera M's house, and the flour mill. A story as brief as the pigeon's flight is over.

Mrs. Zelda Baum once more sits down on the bench outside the house. A peaceful moment at noon. She is alone. The children play, no one knows where. But wherever they are, they can't be heard. She adjusts her reddish brown wig that keeps slipping back. She crosses her arms. The goat continues eating the earliest of the summer apples. The light, reflected off the windowpane behind Mrs. Baum's back, moves over her wig.

Listopadowa is still quiet. In front of the flour mill, near the steps, two wagons stand. Nobody walks by, nobody drives by. The goat shuffles under the apple tree and bleats softly. It is heavy, its belly hangs low, it has eaten too much weed. It raises its long snout, looks pleadingly. One more time it starts moving its ears, lowers its head, bites an apple.

Steam is escaping from the pots placed on the Baums' cast-iron stove. The narrow chimney pipe jutting above the roof steadily lets out a trail of smoke. But the smoke doesn't rise in a clearly defined direction. We must remember: it is noon on a hot and windless day. One time the smoke rises, another time it spreads low over the roof, heading either for the flour mill or for Lwowska, in two completely different directions.

Standing outside Kazimiera M's house in a fixed point from which we watch the sun over Listopadowa and the market square, we notice that the sun has traveled slightly to the right of the pear tree. It seems that it has moved a little, but we aren't sure. Maybe it's the treetop, its leaves limp at noon, that has moved. Probability permits both interpretations.

The door to the tavern—someone released it a moment ago—is swaying. The patron who has just left the tavern totters toward the horses. He experiences some difficulty in tightening up the loose harness on the two grey mares. He pats them tenderly on the necks and sides. He gathers their well-groomed tails, lifts them and slowly lets go. We can see now that such tails are precious and worth hours of grooming. The light sparkles on them as if on water drops. The man seats himself comfortably in the wagon and tries to crack the whip. He drives away in the direction of Hrubieszowska Street.

Just as Rosenzweig's client, unable to crack the whip, is leaving the market square, Rosenzweig, gesticulating and raising his voice, is trying to convince a few young customers that he can't serve them any alcohol, not even beer. He doesn't know them, so how can he be sure their credit is good? An unpleasant and unnecessary disturbance, offensive words and anger that at any moment may lead to a brawl.

With his sleeve Rosenzweig wipes the sweat off his face. The tavern feels stuffy and hot. He adjusts his yarmulke. "This day will surely never end!"

The market square breathes the undulating, expanding air. That's how the Center looks at noon. The Center that is Everything, the Center where the beginning and the end of the world take place. The light plays on the vine leaves covering the houses and stores. A dog runs near the walls of the buildings, it wants to be in shade. The Center is the color of brilliant whiteness.

It's too early for Rosenzweig's pigeons to finish flying. After a row with the young customers, the tavern owner steps outside for a moment. He wants to take a breath of hot but fresh air and glance at the roof and see which of his pigeons are back. He notices that only one is perched there. That makes him truly happy, a reward for the endless hours he spends behind the counter.

It is tempting now to get on one of the hot tin roofs—on the roof of a house or on the flat roof of a store or market stall—on any roof, as long as it's high. (Mr. Baum's fabric store seems too low.) Without taking shoes off—the roof would be too hot—to stand in the most convenient place and look around. One wish grants the pass to this adventure: it is tempting to get on. . . . That's enough. Here we are on the roof of a tall house at the south edge of the market square. The world is limited to the boundaries visibility imposes. But the imagination, free to create details, can expand it once again.

The second sun, the dome of the Town Hall, glows above the Old Town. Along the way, the cross of Saint Augustine's Church. Behind it, the tall building of the law court. The treetops trembling in the light. The green patch of the park to the right of the Town Hall. The red roof tiles in the Old Town and greenish roofs. We can see far from here—very far. But farther on, the greenery is enveloped in haze from which the outlines of hills emerge. And that's the way it is all around, wherever we look. Only the sky is the same everywhere, cloudless and bright as far as we can see.

Here, down below, everything looks magnified. Rosenzweig pours fresh water into a bowl for his pigeons and goes back to the tavern. Someone leaves the tavern, someone else enters. The swinging door is still swaying. Smoke rises from the tavern's chimney.

The stones in the market square are white, as if just taken out of a fire. As if still smoking. But it's only the air that vibrates. The yellow and white dust among the stones is like cooling ashes. The sun bakes the clay pots laid out near the furrier's and the tailor's stalls.

Mr. Hershe Baum strolls in front of his store. He greets

someone. His five children have come running to the store. Sparrows hop on the vines.

If we look carefully, we may see white steam nestling on the brewery roof. The brewery is nearby, but the steam may not be visible from a distance. Everything moves and undulates. Opposite the brewery, among the treetops, the ribbon of smoke rises or spreads like the steam from the brewery roof. It is the smoke from the Baums' stove. We can't see the chimney pipe: maybe this isn't smoke but the breath of the trees at noon.

It's quite probable that in the afternoon the trees breathe deeply. We can see a similar sight in the vicinity of Ogrodowa Street, south of the market square, halfway to the Labunka. Undoubtedly, the high walnut trees are breathing. These are the same trees whose leaves the two policemen, Antoni Wrzosek and Tomasz Romanowicz, were smelling this morning.

Eagerly, we take photographs of both phenomena. Let's stay a while longer in the Center, in the middle where light comes to a focus. Let's wait—something important may happen any minute.

Stroking his beard with his right hand, Mr. Hershe Baum disappears inside his store. Nobody knows where it is cooler. As we know, there's shade in the store. It seems that the air coming in through the open door and the window brings some coolness. The merchant would readily agree that this is only an illusion.

In no time a fiery ball should roll into the market square—maybe like the one we saw in the picture in Rosenzweig's tavern—and set on fire one of the stores or one of the market stalls. In the meantime we take another photograph. In the empty sky a confused dance of the swallows.

Below, a cat cautiously treads the white stones. They are hot, smoke rises above them. We notice—the time is 1:15—that the chimney of Rosenzweig's tavern no longer lets out smoke.

Everything is before us, everything is around us. We have to repeat an obvious and always important truth: we are in the Center. We are at the Beginning and at the End. We are at the place where roads separate in four directions. The roads lead away from the Center and back to it. The movement along the circle.

From Ogrodowa Street a man bikes into the market square. He gets off the bike and, pushing it, approaches the stalls. He most likely encounters his acquaintances because every now and then he stops, shakes hands, talks. He is coming closer and closer to the furrier's and tailor's stalls.

The peculiarity of our observation point: we see more than anybody else. (Only the dome of the Town Hall—the Eye of the Town—sees everything.)

We look in four directions, turning around.

The North:

The market square before us and below. In front, the road leading to Hrubieszowska. The wagon in which Rosenzweig's customer drove away is no longer there. A gentle slope closes the horizon. It is far from here. Before the slope: scattered houses. Strips of fields. Three villages: Lapiguz, Czolki, Sitno. A forest covers the hillside. The sun warms our backs.

The East:

The eastern sector of the market square is closest to us. In it, the fabric store, some other stores and shops, and also Rappaport's bakery. Beyond the market square, a little to the left, the flat roof of the brewery, which now reflects light. Behind the brewery, a school building surrounded by old ash and horse-chestnut trees. And Lwowska, marked by trees growing on its edge. It leads to Kalinowice. Farther, another forest closing the horizon, with villages before it.

The South:

Roofs and trees. Backyards suffocating in the sun. Everything is the same all the way to the end of Ogrodowa. Behind Ogrodowa, wherever we look, meadows. But they aren't only green. Not for the first time this year, the meadows are in bloom. Labunka divides them into two sections: the closer one and the one behind the river. In some places along Labunka, brake and clumps of bushes. Here and there a solitary tree. The mirrors of ponds, trees, then forest.

The West:

The view closest to us is very much like the previous one: gardens, roofs, houses. The western part of the market square is where Rosenzweig's tavern is located. The shiny roof of the bank in the vicinity of the Old Town. And the Old Town illuminated by two suns. (We wonder if the Hasidim are still singing and dancing in front of the Town Hall.) The crosses of the churches and, near the market square, not far from here, the cross of Saint Augustine's Church. The Lvov Gate, which we can't see. Nor can we see the attics or the linden trees outside Attorney Danilowski's office. We can't see the park, where the two suns roll and bounce off the surface of the pond.

We stand facing the market square. The movement along the circle has been completed—we have departed from the source, we have returned to it.

The man with the bike, who a short while ago was near the furrier's and tailor's stalls, has now gone to Rosenzweig's tavern. His bike leans against the wall of the tavern, near the door. Two little boys are squatting and looking at the bike. The swinging door is still.

The color of the sky has been the same since morning. Against the sky the swallows look like black feathers of a bird rent by a hawk. Or like blood from the torn heart of the sky and the clouds. Blood that is reluctant to touch the ground. Other swallows chirp on the telegraph lines.

A siren has sounded from the direction of the Old Town.

Two short signals, perhaps a test. It can be heard at various times and no one knows what that means.

From Lwowska a car drives into the market square. The black body glistens as if water had been poured on it. The driver wearing a green cap waves his hand at somebody. The two boys have abandoned the bike and are running into the middle of the market square. In the meantime the car has disappeared behind the corners of the houses. The boys are still following it.

The siren stops. Mr. Hershe Baum is strolling again in front of his store. It's hard to say whether it's cooler in the store or outside. Mr. Baum's five children are going to a candy booth. Mr. Baum shades his eyes and looks up. He searches the sky for Rosenzweig's pigeons.

From the lane near Baum's store, a man carrying tools on his back walks into the market square. The tools shine. Who is this? It's the Old Wolf. He carries the tools for sharpening knives and patching broken pots. He's been called Wolf because of his restless eyes and unshaved face. Wolf stops near Mr. Baum's store and takes off his bundle. Mr. Hershe Baum walks up to him and both sit on the doorstep of the store.

The last photograph taken on the roof: a ribbon of smoke is rising vertically in the vicinity of Lwowska, before Kalinowice.

The policemen, Antoni Wrzosek and Tomasz Romanowicz, are each at a different place now. Only the hot, sweet sun connects them.

In the corner of the boarded-off barracks area, behind the garrison stable, there's a spot overgrown with lush grass. It is rarely visited—it's at the edges of the barracks, with nothing interesting around. Big, old bushes of lilac and jasmine grow in front of the fence. The wall of the stable with tiny windows and a sloping roof separates this nook from the rest of the barracks area. It's quiet and safe here. Tomasz Romanowicz and his brother, Lieutenant Andrzej Romanowicz, know it. On hot summer afternoons, when time permits, they enjoy lying here, sunning themselves and talking. We can see their uniforms thrown on the grass, belts and boot tops shining in the sun. Tomasz Romanowicz, his hands folded under his head, lies facing the sun. His brother lies on his belly, the side of his face to the sun.

The brothers talk about something, now and again interrupting their conversation with laughter. In fact, if it weren't for the lieutenant's questions or comments, their conversation would be the policeman's monologue. Tomasz Romanowicz is telling his brother about his encounter with Kazimiera M.

That's all that can be said about it.

The second policeman, Mr. Antoni Wrzosek, is walking along the Labunka with his wife Halina and their nearly two-year-old daughter, Katarzynka. The grass is tall here, and it's easy to get entangled in it. From a distance Katarzynka can't be seen in the grass. Insects buzz. Butterflies soar over the meadow. Antoni Wrzosek picks Katarzynka up and comes close to the water. The child bends and reaches forward.

From here, from the bank of the Labunka, the first row of houses in the Old Town is visible, the roofs glistening behind the trees. The rays of the two suns are reflected in the river.

Attorney Walenty Danilowski stands near the window, his arms propped on the windowsill. He has a shirt on but no jacket. The two top buttons of his shirt are undone. It's time to start going to dinner. One more minute, not yet. What is the attorney's wife, Mrs. Maria Danilowski, doing? A troublesome question perhaps, but one that doesn't interest the attorney at all.

Meanwhile, before him, another concert in the linden trees. Baby crows stand at the edge of the nests and flap their undeveloped wings. Propped all the time on the windowsill, the attorney decides to eat dinner in the Central restaurant. With a handkerchief, he wipes sweat from his face and forehead.

The time is 1:23.

The air is dense. The two suns have warmed it up earlier than usual today. The afternoon heat only *seems* to expand it. In fact the air is as dense as morning fog. Another comparison is also possible: the air in February or January may be equally dense. Compressed by frost, it jingles softly. You have only to listen. One more time the attorney wipes the sweat off his face and forehead. The concert in the linden trees goes on. A spot of light on the attorney's face. Right now they jump over a narrow, frozen river. Walek is last, the others are older than he. They let him carry a pole. He has to be careful not to break it. The pole is very long and easy to break. To make matters worse, he can't pull his leg out of the snow. They say something and laugh, turning away from Walek. He'd like to plunge the pole into the snow somewhere or grab one of their caps, twirl it high, then throw it far back behind himself. He can't do that—they wouldn't take him with them again.

The dark wall of the forest before them. It's still far away. Walek stops. He wants to take a rest, to catch a breath. They are about halfway through. The roofs are covered with snow. Here and there smoke rises from a chimney—someone is sending signs of life. All the trees in front of his house look like trees after a fire that burned the leaves. Enough. The trees are dead. The dots of crows at the treetops. The second half of December—every few days a new layer of snow. Far out there, in town, hungry dogs are barking. The red tongues of dogs, the tongues of devils. There are different fires, and there are different hells. Only at night, streaks of fire trail up the sky. It seems that the red tongues of dogs are on fire. Dogs—devils, the phantoms of that winter. After dusk, the doors are bolted, the windows covered. Hungry dogs attack the houses, breathe out smoke and fire. Noise and words that no one has ever heard. Such was Walek's dream. He stops to rest. He hasn't seen the fire-spitting dogs yet. He didn't tell anybody about his dream. Nobody would have believed him. They are calling to him to follow.

The air is dense, compressed by the frost—as if from above, something were pushing it down into the snow. A short, shallow breath, and the lungs are full. The pole feels heavier and more unwieldy. The air jingles softly like distant bells. As far as you can see, no one is riding. The air crackles like sand in an hourglass or snow underfoot. They are smoking cigarettes. Walek breathes in the fragrant smoke. Here on those marshes, on those swampy meadows, during this freezing weather, the smoke is a bit different. Walek doesn't like his grandfather's breath smelling of cigarette smoke or his father's when he sits down in his lap. But today it smells different. Several goldfinches have flown by. The tracks of hares in the snow. Walek squats and, with the tips of his fingers, touches the depressions. The snow in them is somewhat less cold. He must get up and follow the other boys.

"What are you looking for, Walek?"

"I'm just—hares have been here."

Each breath, each deep breath pulls the whole winter into the lungs. The compressed space, like compressed, dense air, tears the body from the inside. The sky is low and, for wintertime, quite bright. It is windless. The air jingles softly. A bright Sunday morning. The first clusters of alders to which they are going stand several minutes away. No one is in a hurry. But Walek would like to be there, be there as fast as possible, be there right now. The dogs, these terrible dogs . . . Maybe it isn't true? Maybe he didn't dream about them?

"Don't look back, Walek. Don't look back. We are almost there. Listen carefully and you'll hear them for sure."

Before the forest, against the snow, a red flame sneaks by. The fox runs, stops. A few leaps and it vanishes behind the nearest trees.

The familiar odor of glue for catching siskins wafts in the air around them. Walek asks them to take the pole from him. It's close to the alders and he's a little ashamed to give it back, but he prefers to walk more freely, run, when he wants, or bend down over something. And the pole gets in the way. He gives it back to Marian. When Marian smiles, his teeth light up his swarthy face.

Now his two hands are free. The partridges flush noisily when he throws a snowball at them. The noise subsides, but it can still be heard. Then it's gone. Walek can't hear them any longer—the partridges sink into the snow like they sink into the grown wheat in the summer, without a trace. Without a trace? The air is vibrating like a chord that has been struck. It radiates. Such a trace two meters above the snow, a transitory reminder that the birds have recently been here. Do they—those that are walking ahead of Walek—see the constantly vibrating air? Do they hear—although it isn't audible, you may always hear it—the beating wings of the partridges that cower behind the juniper bush? Walek doubts that they can see the vibrating air and hear the beating wings. But truly the existence of such phenemona can't be denied. The more Walek doubts that his older friends know about them, the more unshakable his own faith in those phenomena is.

They are close to the first alders. The bare branches, irregularly shaped balls of seed at their tips. The siskins aren't here, but they must be nearby. Walek can smell the glue on the sticks that Marian is holding with care. Walek decides to take the pole again. They walk, scrutinizing the tops of the alders, trying to hear if maybe the siskins are chirping there softly. They can hear the snow crunching and the fragile alder branches breaking under the snow. Soon it will be noon—the bells have sounded in town. A screeching magpie alarms the whole forest. The meadows and the forest are streaked by sunlight. Sun rays bounce off the snow and cross one another many times. Quickened breathing—more and more winter in the lungs. Walek overtakes his friends. He wants to be the first to hear and see the siskins. He is holding the pole, but he doesn't know he has it.

In the snow, the traces of a marten's or a weasel's paws, with hollows left by the claws. They lead to the moss-covered aspen trees. A couple of jackdaws romp in the willow bush. The jackdaws fly off when Walek scares them by waving his hand.

At last they are here. Walek is the first to notice the siskins. They perch quietly, chilled—perhaps in anticipation of the impending annihilation. The rusty-yellow-and-green bellies are ruffled. They peck the alder seeds or hide their beaks in their feathers. Ready to take wing at any moment. They must be approached very cautiously.

This prologue to the mystery of the hunt that is about to begin requires the utmost concentration. Walek is counting siskins. There are nine of them. How many of them will let themselves be caught? What do they know about glue-smeared rods that will adhere to their wings and bellies? The pole with a sticky rod attached to its end is rising up little by little. (A slight stir among the siskins. They leap onto the higher branches.) The pole leans against a thicker branch and for a moment stops. (Don't breathe, don't move an eyelid, listen to the blood coursing through the veins.) Again Walek sees the dog-devils illuminating the town with fire. The dog-devils chase people who run on the streets. The streets are grey from smoke. Together with fire, a cry ascends to the sky. The gluey stick is just now touching the wing. The flutter of the second free wing. The pole with the floundering siskin wanders down.

The remaining eight don't fly away. They are waiting for something—for what? Slowly the boys remove the siskin from the stick. On the snow, the torn-off feathers lie like drops of blood. Walek asks them to let him hold the siskin. They hand him the bird, telling him not to release it. Walek moves the siskin from his right hand to his left, walks to an alder, props his right hand on the trunk and shakes it hard. And he lets the siskin go. All the others have also flown away. The boys look dumbfounded at what has happened.

Walek is running ahead, stumbling, sinking into the snow. They aren't following him, but he can hear their curses. But this doesn't concern Walek anymore, nothing concerns him anymore now.

The attorney is standing in the window, his eyes fixed on some point. Can it be that he once dreamed about dogs raging in town? That the dogs carried people away? This is very baffling. In fact it is unbelievable. Did he dream about them or not? He remembers shaking the alder to scare the siskins away. He remembers coming back home late at night, hungry, chilled, with fingers like icicles. The rest is blurred by fog, by a huge cloud before the eyes that successfully obstructs visibility.

The attorney returns to his desk. The constant hum of the town. The sun slants into the office from the right. It hangs high like before. Its slight shift to the west—is it really a shift?—causes the sun rays to enter the office obliquely, it seems. The rays cross. The second sun, the dome of the Town Hall, continues to shine.

The afternoon is still at its peak. The play of light that no paintbrush will convey. Everything changes in one moment. The attorney raises his eyes and squints. The rays of both suns hit the windowsill. They refract on the windowpanes and, at a new angle, enter the office.

The heated air billows as before over the roofs. Over the tin, over the roof tiles, it rolls down onto the streets, under the feet onto the cobblestones, the dust, and withered grass.

The Hasidim can't be seen in front of the Town Hall. They walked away in an unknown direction. Their white stockings have changed color because of the dust. Who knows—maybe the Hasidim are resting in the shadow of the horse-chestnut trees. Reclining, one hand propped on the grass, the other hand tossing pieces of broken branches into the pond, they watch the circles on the water disperse.

The attorney stares into the corner of the office. Something rustles or stirs there. Nothing can be seen. Flies zoom, land on the desk and on the lamp. Maniek, Marian . . . His last name may have begun with an "M" too. Or maybe with an "N." Or with a "P." It was kind of short. He wore his hair cropped, had a swarthy face, white teeth. In the summer, at the time of haymaking, he liked to sing. After Mass on Sundays, when we went to the forest, he sang. Those songs, short and simple, which I too knew by heart. Jadwiga liked to sing them. What has remained? Where is he, Maniek, whose last name I can't even remember now? And would I recognize him? Fog and confusion in my memory. Nothing is left.

This unexpected recollection of an old friend and play companion about whom he now knew so little put the attorney into a state of pensiveness—or rather of latent sadness. The wheels of a droshky clatter noisily in front of the Dominican church. The attorney doesn't hear that. He is sitting on the edge of a chair, turned towards the back wall of the office. His head is bent down, a strand of hair dangling over his forehead.

He puts a mint drop into his mouth. Several are still left. He goes over today's mail and sorts out the earlier batch. He writes to the more important clients. At this time nobody ever comes to the office. The attorney breathes deeply.

Somewhere far away, in the north, a thunderstorm rolls, but the townspeople don't know about it.

When a cat looks straight at the sun or at the dome of the Town Hall, its pupil narrows. Cats leave the cool of gates and cellars. For a short time they stand in front of the houses, on the lawns, in the warmth of the two suns. Their coats absorb the heat. Sparks discharged by their coats are fragments of the sunrays. Then the cats return to the gates, to the cellars, to the little-known underground life.

As it turns out, the Hasidim are sitting on the benches in the park, under the horse-chestnut trees, close to the pond. Some of them have sat down on the grass. All have loosened up their clothes. One of the Hasidim now and again picks up a discolored chestnut and throws it on the water. Before long the Hasidim will go to dinner, but we don't know yet to which restaurant.

But before that happens the zaddik will intone a new song. The Hasidim will pick up the song's words, and the town will hear singing coming from the park.

Attorney Danilowski seals the envelopes and writes addresses. Soon he will go to dinner as well.

What will happen next?

We have to trust the order of events and things. It is inviolable and the only one right. When we look at the hands of the clock on the Town Hall, we could swear that they are at a standstill. And then, during each passing moment, nothing happens.

We close our eyes. We can hear the pious Hasidim singing a long way off. The air is dense. Let's open our eyes. One, two minutes have passed. The clock readily informs us about it. We can see the attorney scratching his temple with a fingernail. Nothing can be stopped.

Our new photograph:

Blue, black, and white. A stork flying over the town, below

the sun, above the dome of the Town Hall. What will the blue of the sky look like in a photograph? The stork is bound for the meadows, most likely near the Labunka. The wings keep moving. We close our eyes. The wings continue to move. We close our eyes again. A small point vanishing in space.

Let's turn back from the attorney's office. Let's go to Listopadowa, to Lwowska. Let's go to the market square. Let's enter the fire, the smoke, the flood that Mr. Hershe Baum dreamed.

In the market square, as near the attorney's office, it is still early afternoon.

But it is already a different kind of afternoon. The sun that until recently hung at the top of the pear tree has detached itself. And when we stand at the place from which we observed the sun before, we notice that it has really moved to the right. It has moved towards the market square, towards Mr. Hershe Baum's store and Rosenzweig's tavern.

The goat is no longer under the apple tree. Maybe it is plundering someone's garden. Or maybe, hidden from view, it is resting in the shade of a lilac bush. We can't hear its bleating.

We are passing the house in which Kazimiera M lives. We are approaching the flour mill. The sounds of working machines are at first muffled, then louder and louder. Looking for scattered seeds, chickens busy themselves among the piles of horse dung. We don't know if those are the same chickens on which this morning Kazimiera M poured the contents of her chamber pot. At the wall of the mill, flowering dandelions, the leaves wilted from heat. We pick up a leaf: white juice slowly flows. A drop of the juice spreads at the tip of the tongue. How bitter it is!

We are walking on Listopadowa. The flour mill is several steps behind us. A barefoot man, wearing only pants, stands among gooseberry bushes.

The grape balls will swell more and more. The sweetness of the autumn will gather in them. The Baums' children will climb the stakes of the fence and pull on the branches. The whole bush will quiver. After dusk nobody will see them.

In the evening, the policemen, Antoni Wrzosek and Tomasz Romanowicz, also called Romanek, will walk here. Listopadowa will reveal secrets inaccessible to us. The policemen will turn left, into Polna Street. At this time a train will roll by on the edge of town. Sparks will shoot into the air like pieces of a shattered star. The policemen will turn back toward the market square.

Where will Attorney Danilowski be at this time? What will he be doing?

The policemen will walk on Spadek toward the market square. At a leisurely pace, unhastily—but then why should they hurry?—they will pass houses that are falling asleep or already sleeping. Here and there they will spot a lit-up window. Before they come near Kazimiera M's house, they will lower the branches of the cherry tree and pick the fruit. (And if all that doesn't happen?) They will walk in silence, staring down at their feet or looking straight ahead. They will listen to the sounds of the town submerged in darkness.

They will stop in front of Kazimiera M's house. Behind her window they will see a light. The curtains will be closed. Tomasz Romanowicz will say to his colleague that he would love to visit Kazimiera M. "Look, Antoni, only a few steps away . . ."

All that will happen in the evening—if it happens at all. Still several more hours, not quite yet.

Meanwhile we have traveled quite a distance on Listopadowa. Behind us a vine laces the wall. Each step—not only our steps—is a new word in the Book of the Day that is being created before everyone's eyes. We must read it word by word and ask what each word means. The book conceals nothing. Everything is visible, as on a July morning.

The sun is above us and around us—here, on Listopadowa, but also in the market square. But who knows that today, as on every sunny day, the second sun, the dome of the Town Hall, shines as well? Do its rays reach both Listopadowa and the market square? This is not so certain.

We are approaching Hrubieszowska Street. It seems that is where Rosenzweig's customer rode away, trying unsuccessfully to crack the whip.

The sun is on our legs and backs. We sweat profusely, but after a while forget about it. Some gooseberries from a roadside bush go into our mouths, followed by an unripe, sour apple. Children are playing in front of the house that we pass by. They stare at us with the greatest curiosity. It doesn't last long—they are too preoccupied with their own affairs.

Someone shuts the window noisily. Sparrows shoot away from the sand. A windowpane in the shade—it doesn't reflect any light.

(Has Walenty Danilowski left his office yet?)

We are on Hrubieszowska. Neither the market square nor the brewery opposite the Baums' house can be seen from here. The tin roof of the flour mill on Listopadowa is visible. A second mill stands a short way off and a third one stands on Spadek. The market square is close by.

It's so close that we can guess what's going on there now, even though we don't know for sure because we can't see anything from Hrubieszowska. Some patrons are leaving Rosenzweig's tavern, others are arriving. The bike is standing against the wall. In the sun the horses are getting restless. Rosenzweig is drawing beer. Two wagons going in opposite directions pass one another at the end of Lwowska. In front of the brewery a goat is grazing.

Soon it will be two o'clock. The rays of both suns, the mobile and immobile, reach into every corner in town. Hrubieszowska Street is yellow with dust. Each day, each summer day, there is more dust. We may try to explain this phenomenon. When sun rays explode, they leave traces. The dust comes from shattered rays that continually fall down. Sometimes their quiet rustling can be heard. We walk over the sun, the sun is under our feet.

We are coming to the road which Rosenzweig's customer took. Does he know he rode over the sun? Riddles, questions. On the road we see wagon ruts and the tracks of horses' hooves.

Let's stop here for a moment and look ahead. Before us we have the market square. We walk slowly for a few minutes. The sun has moved farther west, toward the Old Town. It has passed Mr. Hershe Baum's store, Rosenzweig's tavern, Saint Augustine's Church. It has passed the market square.

We stop. Something is happening. Something is ending. We see a flock of Rosenzweig's pigeons circling low over the market square. It is two o'clock. In a short time the pigeons will land on a heated roof. How long have they been flying? Eight hours? Perhaps.

The market square is white—white from the sun. The air pulsates over the pavement. Four wagons are standing in front of Rosenzweig's tavern. The bike is leaning against the wall. A car is disappearing into Lwowska. Mr. Hershe Baum, his arm propped on the wall of his store, looks ahead, most likely at Rosenzweig's pigeons, which are still in the air. (What about Mr. Hershe Baum's pigeons?) The market square is empty. The swallows are nowhere to be seen or heard. Where are they?

Maybe now the swallows are rinsing their wings in the pond. Maybe the Hasidim see them. A photograph that we certainly won't take: all the swallows from town are rinsing their feathers in the pond. The sun bounces off the water and leaps—once up, once down.

But this doesn't happen in the market square. In the market square the vines, limp and dusty—also covered with sun dust—provide less and less protection from the sun. Mr. Hershe Baum puts a padlock on the door to the fabric store and makes his way toward the booth selling lemonade. The sparrows have left the vines. It's dangerously hot there now.

Mr. Hershe Baum hasn't locked his store for long. We can see him come back from the booth and open the padlock.

A child has uttered a loud cry. Suddenly there's silence.

Around the stalls lie crushed cherries and gooseberries. They give off a sweetly sour smell.

Mrs. Zelda Baum passes the first houses on Lwowska and walks into the market square. She is going to her husband. She will take his place while he heads home to eat. It happens that way every day. After the meal, Mr. Hershe Baum will return to his store to do business. Right now they are still talking. Mr. Baum tells his wife about the kinds of fabric he has sold today. It seems he hasn't sold much. Mrs. Zelda Baum nods with understanding.

Mr. Hershe Baum takes off his yarmulke and with his fingers combs his hair. He wipes his face on a handkerchief. His wife is already seated behind the counter. She adjusts an uncomfortable wig, looking intently at the mirror. Mr. Baum puts on the yarmulke and leaves the store. "I'll be back in half an hour." Busy with her wig, Mrs. Zelda Baum doesn't respond.

The merchant is already on Lwowska. Although hungry, he decides to stop over at the refreshment booth. He is drinking soda water. Two of his daughters are running to meet him. He picks up the younger one. But where are his three sons? They can't be seen on Listopadowa.

Close to his house, Mr. Hershe Baum stops for a moment. He lets go of his daughters' hands. He raises his head and searches the sky for the pigeons. Very high, in the clear sky, several dark dots are moving. He rubs his hands with glee. "They are still flying." He disappears behind the corner of the shed, opens the door and enters the house.

Before Mr. Hershe Baum manages to take off his vest and wash his face, his two daughters run out of the house. They gather some green apples from under the apple tree behind the gate. Munching on the apples and singing something at the same time, they walk on Listopadowa in the direction of Lwowska.

The grass in front of the brewery looks withered. The sun has dried the moisture. Since morning, the smell of fermenting barley and yeast has permeated the air.

Another wagon departs from the flour mill heading for Hrubieszowska.

Kazimiera M comes back from the footpath she took to Spadek. The hallway is dark, the floor and stairs squeak. Her upstairs room is filled with the suffocating odor of perfume.

With a vigorous movement of the hand, Kazimiera M opens the window that she had left slightly ajar. She leans on the windowsill, resting the weight of her whole body on her hands. She raises her arms, squints. The sunrays wander on her face. Kazimiera M turns her head toward Listopadowa. The flat roof of the brewery shows no trace of steam.

Standing on tiptoes, Kazimiera M leans out the window. Her face is turned to the sun, her head slightly raised. The light reflected off the open window sparkles and bends in her brown hair.

It's too warm. For a moment Kazimiera M puts her hand in her hair. Her skin is hot. In that short moment every part of Kazimiera M's body is as hot as her hand. Unexpectedly her back shivers, or maybe twitches. She unbuttons her green and white dress and slips it off her pale shoulders. She opens the horn clasp and places it on the windowsill.

In the light Kazimiera M's hair looks as if it were inlaid with glittering gems. We had to repeat it.

The blue panties pinch the skin on her hips. Kazimiera M puts her hand inside the dress and pulls the panties down a bit. She feels some relief.

From under the lilac bush a rooster crows wearily. Someone is pulling a cart on Listopadowa. The wooden wheels, tin bands around them, rattle noisily. Kazimiera M turns her head and opens her eyes a little. The cart rides away. She closes her eyes—the cart can't be seen, its rattling grows quiet.

The rattling subsides.

Mr. Hershe Baum turns the key in the lock, takes the key out and hangs it on the nail in the shed. He goes out onto the street. He raises his head. The pigeons are still flying. He walks slowly. Soon he will come to Lwowska.

Kazimiera M disappears into her apartment. She pours water into a basin and dips her fingers in it. She takes her hands out of the water, shakes the drops off. Her fingers are still dripping. Kazimiera M wets her cheeks, lips, forehead, and eyes. She repeats all those activities.

She doesn't know whether Attorney Danilowski will pay her a visit this evening. She would like to know that. Frequently, the attorney's visits are a surprise for which she is unprepared, just as Romanowicz's are. Romanowicz visits her less often but always at the wrong time. Attempts to set those matters right have failed. Kazimiera M's predicament is something of a misfortune.

The room is very hot. Kazimiera M takes off her dress and hangs it folded on the arm of a chair. She lies down on the bed. She would like to rest a while.

The stream of sunlight that pours into her room through the window is directed at the east wall. As a result of its afternoon movement, the sun gets closer to the Old Town. The beam of light bathes Kazimiera M's back and the hair strewn across her shoulders. An exciting, salty taste of hot skin.

Kazimiera M slips her left hand into her blue panties and delicately scratches the skin of her buttock. While she's doing that, she pulls the panties down because the elastic keeps pinching her. It should be noted that the panties are trimmed with a delicate white lace. She drops her left hand, brushing the floor with her fingers.

Mrs. Zelda Baum is returning from the store. A woman walks with her. They stop in front of the gate. Mrs. Baum gestures for them to sit on the bench in front of the house. But they don't sit down. What are they talking about? We don't know.

Mr. Hershe Baum's pigeons fly lower now. Who can count the hours they have been flying? Amazing perseverance—they have been flying since early morning.

Kazimiera M's back heaves. She's breathing quietly and evenly. Her hand doesn't move. She seems to have fallen asleep. What is she dreaming of?

Mrs. Zelda Baum covers her mouth and yawns. The woman she's talking to, her hands folded on her chest, yawns too, as if mimicking Mrs. Baum. She picks an apple off the ground, and, on a path beaten in the grass, walks towards Spadek. Mrs. Baum takes the key off the nail.

Her children aren't near the store. She turns the key in the lock and opens the door.

The sky has been the same since morning—cloudless, maybe now a little clearer. Perhaps the two suns have brightened it up.

The door to Rosenzweig's tavern opens and a customer appears in it. He rests his hands and, after a while, also his head on the wall of the tavern. Stumbling, he walks to Gminna.

On the hot roof of the tavern—the sun is still shining—the pigeons are resting. They roost on wooden ladders, their wings limp. And suddenly, one after another, they fly to the ground, to drink water out of a bowl that Rosenzweig has placed in the shade.

We should be alert. We should painstakingly record everything so that nothing is missing from the Book. What we can't ascertain with our own eyes we should bring to life by the law of probability.

In Mr. Hershe Baum's store two new customers are looking at the merchandise. The store owner pulls off the shelves the rolls of fabric that they point at. The women finger the fabric and ask the price. Mr. Baum informs them that in no other store will they find merchandise of such good quality at such reasonable prices.

The sun, which slowly wanders toward the Old Town, is still present in Mr. Hershe Baum's store. The early afternoon deprives one of breath and makes the body torpid. The merchant wipes a trickle of sweat off his forehead. A small mirror standing on the counter reflects light. The two customers are leaving the store. Mr. Baum bows and recommends his store for the future. The women disappear through one of the gates at the southern edge of the market square.

Mr. Baum's Persian butterflies are landing on the brewery roof. Today they were flying longer than he expected. After a while, thirsty and hungry, they fly onto the shed.

Not a single wagon stands in front of Rosenzweig's tavern. Most patrons have left and the tavern is almost empty. Rosenzweig is not behind the counter. Maybe he is counting pigeons. The patrons sit in silence and smoke cigarettes. The tavern is full of smoke. The smoke blends with the smell of male sweat, beer, vodka, and slivovitz. All day, every day. The same movement of the damp rag that wipes the top. The same two-pronged fork that searches for herring in the glass jar. It is the essence of things, of events. The eternal metaphysics drawn from impenetrable darkness.

In his apartment in the back of the tavern, Rosenzweig is lying, very tired, on his bed. A few minutes stolen from the tavern, during which he can close his eyes.

Attorney Danilowski closes the door of the Central restaurant. The clock hand on the Town Hall is constantly moving forward. With his tongue he tries to remove a piece of meat stuck between his teeth. Soon he will find himself opposite the Town Hall. Walking straight ahead all the time, he will pass Akademicka Street in under three minutes. There he will stop and look around. He will stand before Saint Thomas's Church and the two rows of trees that lead to the court building.

The Hasidim are entering a kosher restaurant. They are cheerful. They let the zaddik go first, then they close the glass door. The uproar subsides. A curtain stirs on the door. Like the zaddik, they gesture with their hands. They eye his finger, it points upward. Only they know what this gesture means.

The cabdriver is leaning on the railing. From here the light of the second sun, the dome of the Town Hall, can be seen as it falls softly on the horse's hair. The slanting rays are very hot—the dome is only several meters away. On the railing, between the cabdriver's hands, ants walk. It seems that the driver hasn't noticed them. But the Eye of the Town certainly sees them.

The sun is now behind Morando Street, behind the cabdriver, behind the Town Hall. The shadow of the droshky has disappeared on the other side of the Town Hall. The wheels that were rattling on the pavement have grown silent.

Attorney Walenty Danilowski is on Akademicka. He stops, looks at the park, at Saint Thomas's Church. The shade of the trees growing in front of the church encircles him. He buttons up his jacket and is already behind the gate.

"In the name of the Father, and of the Son, and of the Holy . . ." A big drop of holy water trickles down his forehead and further down the furrow between his cheek and nose. The attorney wipes the drop on the sleeve of his jacket, its smeared trace remaining on his face a while longer. In front of the attorney, in the pews, old women run their fingers over the wooden beads of rosaries: "... thy kingdom come, thy will be done ..." The attorney covers his ears with his hands. Isn't the silence in the church deep enough? He looks at the dark grain of the wooden benches. For sure, the rays from the dome of the Town Hall don't reach here. If they do, there's very little of that light. The attorney places both hands on the bench. A woman who has just come in sits down by him. In the paintings the figures of the saints are hard to make out. The attorney stares at a painting, trying to see who it represents. A halo above the head, a pale face . . . but the details are obscure.

He passes his fingers over the bench—his fingertips feel every nodule. He rests his finger in a cavity and pushes. The wood withstands the pressure. The attorney presses more forcefully. The cavity yields to the thrust of the fingernail. Black dust rises from it. The attorney covers his ears again. A vast silence, enclosed by the wall, reverberates off the vault and the floor. The attorney moves his hands. He can hear his hair rustle, a dull buzzing as if from a seashell. ". . . And forgive us our trespasses as we forgive those who trespass against us ..." The grating sound of the metal doorknob. The door opens noisily. The beam of light cast across the middle of the church stops at the opposite wall. All that happens in an instant—the beam shortens, the door closes. The attorney manages to notice that the painting on which the beam has rested represents Saint Joseph.

He bends his head. Only now does he notice how stuffy it is here because of the smell of the flowers. "Thou shalt have no other gods before me. . . ." With his fingers he massages his temples. He opens his mouth wide. His nostrils dilate. The dizzying smell of flowers makes breathing difficult. He remembers that the same jugs full of flowers stood all through the summer and autumn before the altar of the church which the Danilowskis attended. In the spring, women brought armloads of white or purple lilacs, blooming jasmine, and later, lilies and lupine. . . . Now the attorney sees the jugs and thick glass vases with flowers. He can't breathe, his lungs are full, but that isn't enough. He thrusts his fingernail deeper into the depression in the bench, closes his eyes tightly. "The ninth: Thou shalt not covet thy neighbor's wife. . . ." Under his eyelids he sees a flickering brightness. Someone comes in again and another sunbeam lights Saint Joseph's face. God rest their souls, the attorney prays—rest whose souls?—he beats his chest. He can hear a supplication to the Virgin Mary. It is the prayer of a woman who sits in front of him. "Blessed Mother, let him come back as quickly as . . ." The attorney looks at the woman's grey hair, braided and carefully tied at the back of her head. The woman's head is bent, her hands clasped above her hair, elbows at rest on the pew. "Who shall I ask, Blessed Mother, if not . . ." "In the name of the Father and of the Son and of the Holy Spirit. Amen."

The attorney touches his forehead and his shoulders with the tips of his fingers. The dizzying smell of flowers makes his head spin. He walks out of the pew, puts a coin into the collection box. A big drop of holy water runs down his forehead, down his face. He wipes it off with a handkerchief. The large door creaks. The coolness of the metal doorknob, the dome of the Town Hall, the sun slowly losing its earlier brightness. He squints. The birds chirp in the trees in front of the church.

The attorney hastily crosses to the other side of Akademicka Street. He enters the shade under the trees alongside the avenue that leads to the court. The avenue is empty.

The sun moves gradually toward Szczebrzeszyn and Zwierzyniec. The second sun, the dome of the Town Hall, shines more faintly.

Tomasz Romanowicz jumps over the wooden fence of the barracks and is already on Lubelska Street. He brushes and smooths his pants. He combs his hair. Now he will go home. Dinner, then afternoon rest before the next night duty. What will happen tonight? This is a premature worry. Nothing can be predicted.

He walks in the direction of the Town Hall. Alert, he scans the street. The bikes and wagons make a grating noise. The iron rims of the wheels move slowly and systematically—as slowly and systematically as the sun and the hands of the clock atop the Town Hall. The policeman disappears. He has entered one of the houses he was passing by.

In the meantime the Hasidim are finishing dinner. In a few minutes they will leave the restaurant. Slowly—there's no need to hurry—they drink compote. They savor it and smack their lips. The zaddik holds a glass. He raises it to the level of his eyes and turns it toward the light. The compote is light red. Tiny particles of fruit float in it. It smells of sour cherries and gooseberries.

The zaddik brings the glass to his mouth. Two, three, four big swallows. His larynx rises and falls. He puts the empty glass aside. Reddish drops flow in the furrows that run from the corner of his mouth down to his chin.

Suddenly all of them stand up. One of the Hasidim, red-haired, thin and tall, pays the bill for dinner. The owner of the restaurant bows to such unusual guests and opens the glass door. With a benevolent smile, the zaddik leaves the restaurant first.

The Hasidim are in the shade of the Town Hall. The second sun, with the dome hanging over its top, begins to wane. They can't decide where to go. Return to the park? Sit down on a bench somewhere? Doze in the afternoon sun? The zaddik decides they will go to the Jewish cemetery. They ask directions and leave the square in front of the Town Hall. They walk toward the New Town.

Meanwhile, after dinner, the tired policemen, Antoni Wrzosek and Tomasz Romanowicz, are asleep. Antoni Wrzosek's wife, Halina, told Katarzynka to be quiet. The policeman is sleeping on his back. Every now and then his fitful snoring can be heard.

Tomasz Romanowicz is also sleeping—in the garden, behind the house, on the grass, in the shade of the cherry tree. He sleeps on his belly, his hands clasped under his head, his legs spread wide apart. He has on grey pants and a blue shirt. Above him hang branches loaded with fruit that is like stars, like constellations of cherry stars. Their skins glisten. The sun is reflected in the cherries as if in innumerable mirrors, each a sun in miniature, reflecting innumerable rays. Are they cherries then or constellations of stars? Or perhaps suns?

Romanowicz's sleep is deep and sound. What does he know about astral occurrences, which are as important as all other events and phenomena that take place above his head? And do we know any more than he does? Maybe Romanowicz is dreaming about those constellations. Let's wish him beautiful dreams.

A flock of chirping starlings alights on the tree under which Romanowicz is sleeping. There is a lot of activity in the branches. The starlings hop and peck on the stars/sun/cherries. Tomasz Romanowicz turns uneasily onto his side. He puts his right hand, which lay motionless on the grass, on his thigh. High—in the highest branches—the chirping becomes more intense. The policeman sighs, says something in his dream, but except for the starlings no one can hear him.

The sun keeps moving farther and lower.

To see. To be. To remember. To record scrupulously. One more photograph. And then another one. To follow what disappears. Not to miss anything.

The pious Hasidim have passed the Lvov Gate. They are close to the Jewish cemetery. It would take one candy drop to cover the distance (the drop could be mint, of course) if one of the Hasidim put it now into his mouth. But the Hasidim have no candy drops. They are walking in twos and threes.

Here is a photograph for the album: the Hasidim against the Lvov Gate. A little farther, the waning second sun—the dome of the Town Hall. Behind the dome, slightly to the left, lowering itself centimeter by centimeter, the sun which we have seen over the town since morning.

The starlings have flown away from above Tomasz Romanowicz's head. He is still asleep on his side, his hands again clasped under his head. The scent of grass, the scent of flowers, the strong scent of the soil. From the scarred cherries, juice dribbles on the grass and on the policeman.

The Hasidim are gone from the Lvov Gate. As before, they are walking in twos and threes.

Over the Old Town small clouds of smoke are visible. Unnoticeably they dissolve in the air. One moment they are here, another they are gone. The second sun, the dome of the Town Hall, not long ago white hot, is losing its brilliance. Does the smoke from the fading sun turn into clouds?

The windows are open in the court building. Behind them there's silence, as if no one were there. On the edge of the roof two jackdaws try to outshout one another. A black dog with a cutoff tail runs out from the bushes and sniffs the lamppost and the trees.

It is still hot—hot all the time. A sweet, lazy afternoon. In the Old Town the doors to the fabric stores are open. Silk, linen, lace, calico, wool. Watchmakers sit in their shops. And the droshkys have returned. Unfortunately, they have no customers. Only occasionally will someone ask for a ride to the New Town.

We look up. The small clouds, which a few minutes ago were dissolving around the Town Hall, have vanished. Over the Old Town the sky is unblemished by white. Now and then flocks of swallows flush off the wires and out of the nests. A butterfly as big as a swallow shakily flies away toward the park.

The droshky has jolted twice in front of the Town Hall. The horses briskly pass the synagogue. The droshky turns left, approaches Lubelska, and disappears behind the houses and the trees.

The dome of the Town Hall no longer serves as the second sun. Any obscurity, which up till now may have surrounded the waning of the second sun, has ended in a generally visible conclusion. There is the Town Hall, the clock, the dome. There is one sun over and behind the town. There are fewer sun rays, less light. Now the dome is a metal basin suspended high up. The Eye of the Town.

What is going on in the park?

The waning of the second sun effects easily noticeable changes in the pond. From behind the tall horse-chestnut trees we can see the sun, which has moved farther away. The surface of the pond isn't as luminous as it was at noon. And the sun doesn't bounce off the surface like a ball. The sun is too far to bounce off, return to the point of permanent suspension (is it really permanent if we say that the sun has moved farther away, and in a little while we'll say that it has moved even farther away?) and then come close to the surface. So—because the sun rays don't reach here, the duckweed is dark green. The pond breathes, but the breath is more shallow. And the breath of the park is more shallow. The ducks bury their heads in the water. The Eye of the Town, the dome of the Town Hall, sees everything.

We would like to see a fraction of what it sees. We would know where the droshky has gone. And where the dog with a cutoff tail is. We would see what Kazimiera M is doing right at this moment. And Mr. Rosenzweig and Mr. Baum. We would learn where the Baums' sons are. Who enters and leaves Rosenzweig's tavern. Whether the Hasidim have reached the Jewish cemetery yet. What is happening in the linden trees in front of the attorney's office. Whether the goat has come back to the apple tree. (Maybe it is bleating.) And whether the flour mill on Listopadowa has already been closed. We would have to ask the dome of the Town Hall, which sees everything. The Eye of the Town.

We are in the park alone. It's quiet. The ducks dive under the water and study the anatomy of the pond. From the bottom, fish come to the surface. They watch the branches of the birch tree overhanging the water. Occasionally a fly zooms by. Then we see a fin move impatiently and the duckweed sway. But soon—when the fly disappears—everything is the way it was before. The fish watches the branches or settles at the bottom.

All the time the sky is high and still bright. Again a flock of swallows shoots up over the roofs. The droshky comes back on Lubelska. It stops near the first houses of the Old Town. The cabman leaves the horses and walks off somewhere.

The Hasidim are at the Jewish cemetery. It's dark here, as if in a dense forest. Sometimes lovers come here in the evening. The smell of grass and herbs. In the brake, waist-high here and there, white stockings glimmer. It's easy to get entangled in the grass. The Hasidim disperse in the cemetery. Sometimes one of them says something loudly. The voices rarely break the darkness. They read the Hebrew inscriptions unknown to most residents of the town. The zaddik bends down and wrinkles his forehead. He reads word after word. The Hasidim's white stockings are like fireflies at night.

One by one, the Hasidim go inside the Jewish cemetery. Occasionally, someone retreats. A wild pigeon coos high up in the branches—as if under the sun. It's cool. A pair of white legs here, a pair there. They are more and more difficult to see. The Hasidim walk away. Their silhouettes are now barely visible.

Except for a few, the rest—it seems—can no longer be seen. One of them may shout something or at least it may only seem so. The last of the white stockings vanish as if the fireflies had hidden themselves away. No one is here; the Jewish cemetery is empty. The Hasidim have gotten entangled in the brake, from which they can't free themselves. Or what seems more certain, they have sunk under the ground, under the tombs.

Or maybe the Hasidim haven't been here at all? Maybe they haven't. It wasn't certain that they danced and sang in front of the Town Hall, after they had appeared on Morando Street, the bridge of light. All the events we witness are certain and obvious but the presence—the existence—of the Hasidim is and was uncertain. (Similarly uncertain was the white steam sliding from the brewery roof, down along the wall and onto the grass.)

The Jewish cemetery is empty and quiet in the dark. The pigeon is cooing. It's difficult to say if someone walked here or not. The herbs smell bitter. There's mint, a lot of mint. Walking deeper into the cemetery, we can hear only faint sounds of the town. Up among the leaves, a crack lets in a sharp beam of light. No one is here.

In the market square of the New Town, the stones are cooling. Slowly they recover their light grey color. The cats can walk on them without fear. At night—will we see that?—when the cats' coats start discharging sun rays, the stones will glow for a short time, and then the glow will die. Someone will say that dogs have left a bone and it shines. Or maybe no one will notice the stones with sun rays scattered on them.

Rosezweig's pigeons are most likely in the pigeon coop. Behind the opening in the southern wall looms the darkness of the garret.

The daylong exchange of clientele at Rosenzweig's tavern becomes more intense at certain times. It seems that the moment has come when even the most persistent customers are going away. Every now and then several of them leave. Some will drive away in wagons, others will loiter in the market square. But the new patrons are arriving. Those, as we can expect, will stay in the tavern until closing time. A wagon with four men comes. Officers enter the tavern. They probably are in this part of town by accident. Some teenage boys come for wine. The company is in the best of spirits. The officers unbutton their uniforms. It's stuffy.

Cywia Rosenzweig, the tavern owner's wife, brings out pots of steaming meat. Its odor fills the place.

Roza, the Gypsy woman, strolls in the market square, waiting for those who would like to have their fortunes told. She peeks into the still-opened stores, leans onto the stalls. Hands folded across her chest, she rocks back and forth. Her skirts move to the rhythm of her body. Two moons dangle from her ears.

From her apron pocket she withdraws a handful of small coins. She tosses them from hand to hand. Someone might think she is playing with gold. She places the coins on the stall counter. A few coins roll in different directions. She stops them and gathers them together. Then she pushes them with her forefinger, groups them according to size, and counts. She asks someone for a cigarette. After she has it, she asks for the light. "Would you like to have your fortune told, Sir?" But the man walks away. Roza inhales the smoke and slowly lets it out through her mouth and nose. Her face in the smoke looks as if it were surrounded by clouds. From behind the clouds the two moons shine.

Rocking her hips, the Gypsy passes the people arranging pots on a wagon. With each breath the crimson roses on her blouse rise over her large breasts. She strides into the street, looks back one more time. Cigarette smoke encircles her head.

Mr. Hershe Baum bends over a pulled-out drawer. In the drawer, coins shine. A pair of scissors lies in the middle, among the change. The scissors weigh down a few bills of small value and a sheet of paper for calculations. Mr. Baum stares at the contents of the drawer and, like every day, estimates his earnings. (It is also a moment of concentration before the tedious act of adding up the coins—of adding up the moments behind the counter, the centimeters of silk, the tremors of the sun, the trickles of sweat flowing down the face, and also the words that have been said today.)

From the west, through the open door and window, sun rays enter in a straight line. Mr. Hershe Baum puts the money on the countertop—first the bills, then the coins. He gathers the coins and spreads them on the counter with a flattened palm, careful not to let them fall on the floor.

The Gypsy woman is near Rosenzweig's tavern. She unfolds her scarf, furls it over her head and onto her back. The long and twisted fringes swing to the side. She pulls on the corners of the scarf, removes her hair from under it, and shakes her head. The hair covers part of the design on the scarf.

Rosenzweig's customer, who has just left the tavern, is now coming back. Roza walks toward him. They meet near the window. "You won't begrudge the Gypsy woman some money. I can see you won't. You're still young, but I know what you'll do and what you'll become. Give me your left hand, from the heart, like that. Straighten out your fingers. Now listen to what I'll say. Your life is like wind. You'll go somewhere. Yes, your hand says so. A trip awaits you—where, I don't know. Great water, the river or the sea, you'll see yourself, but not now, not yet. You have had women—there will be more of them, but you have already loved. How old were you then?" She looks him straight in the eye. From the beginning of her monologue, the man's face has shown great curiosity and attention (even concentration and some pain). The man notices the moon-shaped earrings dangling below the Gypsy's ears. "You won't return where you'd like to return, and you won't die where you'd like to die. You'll live a beautiful and long life. . . ." Roza has freed her client's hand, although it seems that he has withdrawn it. He takes a bill out of his pocket. Roza hastily closes her fingers on the money.

The man pushes hard on the door to the tavern. The door opens, closes, opens again and closes for good, twice slamming the frame—for the first time today. The Gypsy woman has propped her elbows on the windowsill. She watches her client, who, standing before the bar, drinks one glass of vodka and follows it with another.

Mr. Hershe Baum writes down columns of figures on a sheet of paper. Into his pocket he puts the coins he has already counted. Someone's shadow flits by the store—he doesn't notice whose. The merchant will stay at the store another half hour, or maybe longer.

Roza crosses the market square at an angle. She takes a cigarette out of her skirt pocket and lights it. In her left hand she clutches the bill she has just received. The fringes of her navy blue scarf move with each step she takes. The moons, clipped to her ears, also move. She puts the bill into her pocket. Her fingers encounter crumbled tobacco.

The sparrows have returned to the vines that entwine the fabric store. Quiet chirping can be heard in the market square.

Mr. Hershe Baum has just finished calculating today's profits. With his finger he wipes the tip of his tongue on which some bitter residue from the pencil has gathered. On his lower lip the residue has left a purple stain.

Children are playing in front of the market stalls. Mr. Hershe Baum stands in the door to his store and looks at the opposite wall of the market square. The tin roof hides half of the sun disk. When the second half disappears as well, he will close the door and the windows of his store. Now he shakes his pocket, heavy with coins.

A car has gone slowly in the direction of Hrubieszowska Street, its motor working noisily. It has left blue clouds of exhaust fumes. The slanting sunrays lighten the driver's cream-colored jacket. The black body of the car reflects them.

The pavement in the market square, with its smooth and pale grey stones, is still warm. Dust, sand, and sundust blow over it. The air is also warm because the sun is still shining.

Roza walks toward Spadek along the path lined with sunflowers. She passes the fabric store. On her shoulder she carries purple lace, interwoven with gold thread. We take a photograph of Roza at the moment when she turns her head back. The swinging moon sends faint light from under her left ear. The last bees circle the sunflowers. Roza's shoulders and the hems of her three skirts brush against the leaves. We can hear a quiet rustling.

All the time Mr. Hershe Baum has been standing in the door to the fabric store and looking ahead. He either looks at the sun coming down or at the market square.

The face of each sunflower is turned west. Roza has disappeared on the other side of the path. The dome of the Town Hall, the all-seeing Eye of the Town, sees her.

It also sees the Baums' three sons.

Kazimiera M has woken up. Her sleep wasn't planned, but it was very desirable—the debt paid to the night before, and at the same time, part of it owed to the coming night. Kazimiera M has slept less than two hours. She sits on the edge of the bed and covers her face with her hands. Her tangled hair falls over them.

The pinching panties make themselves felt again. Kazimiera

M pulls them up a bit higher with the fingers of both hands. Her eyes are still closed. She doesn't move.

The market square is already darker. The half of the sun disk that up till now has been showing from behind the tin roof has hidden on its other side.

The rooster's robust crowing has brought Kazimiera M back to life. She rests her arm on the wall, opens her eyes, and raises her head higher. A mirror propped up on a vase stands in front of her. Since it is separated from her by a table and a chair, it doesn't show her whole figure. Kazimiera M turns her head both ways and looks at her neck and hair. And at the three small sunflowers. Two of them are turned towards the window, the third touches the mirror with its petals. Kazimiera M feels the blood throb in the artery on the side of her neck. The yellow petal of a sunflower is falling on the table.

The pear tree between the Baums' house and the house in which Kazimiera M lives has uncurled its leaves. We don't know if that happened at the moment the sun hid behind the roof. The dark green and glossy leaves absorb the last rays with their whole surface. (That may be the beginning of the next chapter of the Book.)

Kazimiera M is putting on the green dress with white flowers. Starting at the bottom, she fastens the buttons, except for the last two at the top. Now she squats and buckles the straps of her sandals. Black hairs can be seen on her legs.

Kazimiera M moves a tall chair with an arched back near the window. She props the oval mirror on the window frame and sits down before it. Immediately she stands up: she has forgotten the comb. The arduous activity of combing begins. Kazimiera M always combs her hair carefully. She treats this activity like a ritual repeated several times a day. Right now we can see her bend her head down, turn it to the side, and brush the hair off her forehead.

The goat is wandering along Listopadowa. Occasionally it nibbles at the grass or moves its tail. Its udder is filled with milk. Flies don't pester it anymore.

(Is Mr. Hershe Baum already closing the doors and the window to the fabric store? Where is Roza, the Gypsy woman? What are the tavern owner, Rosenzweig, and his wife Cywia doing? What are the two officers talking about?)

It's quiet at the brewery. The front gate and, a little farther, the side gate have been locked. The watchman sits on an overturned barrel. Two dogs come close to his legs but right away run off to nose someplace else.

All the wagons have driven away from the flour mill. Only the hens scratch the horse manure there. Little boys sit on the steps and swing their legs in the air.

The early evening lull fills the air on Listopadowa. From the west, through the branches, slanting rays descend. The long shadows of the trees. Among them, the moving, long shadows of the hens.

The roofs blaze in the early evening light. They are covered with tin, tile, thatch. Sparks jump in the welds. It's the sundust, pouring down all day, that sparkles. The same sparkling sundust comes down the roof tiles.

Meanwhile the goat is rambling in front of Kazimiera M's house. On the gravel it leaves traces of its hooves. It sniffs the wall with its wet nose and rubs itself on the corner of the house. It doesn't notice Kazimiera M combing her hair in the window.

Out of a sack Mrs. Zelda Baum takes a handful of straw. She asks her children to gather it in front of the mill or in the market square. She removes the stove lids, and through the opening, she puts straw and dry sticks into the stove. Then quickly, one after another, she slides the stove lids back in place. She remembers to leave a small crack to let the fresh air flow in.

Kazimiera M sticks her head out of the window. She is looking in the direction of the market square, in the direction of the Old Town. She sees the Eye of the Town, the dome of the Town Hall.

The Eye of the Town can certainly notice that the pipe of the Baums' cast-iron stove is letting out smoke—for the third time today. Maybe the last.

The Eye of the Town also sees Mr. Hershe Baum closing the door to his store. High, at the top of the door and right above the doorstep, he fastens two padlocks. He turns the key in the lock under the doorknob. The windows of the fabric store are already shut. Mr. Hershe Baum carefully closes the solid wooden shutters. (Startled sparrows, like every day, fly away from the vines.) On the shutters he puts iron bars and at their ends fastens padlocks slightly smaller than the ones on the door.

Old Wolf cuts across Ogrodowa Street. Where did he leave the bundle with the tools? He doesn't carry anything on his back.

With satisfaction, Mrs. Zelda Baum watches the flames flare up. The dry sticks have caught fire, so now larger chips should be placed in the stove. When they start burning as well, Mrs. Zelda Baum will prepare supper. Then she will heat water for the children to wash. ("But where are my boys?")

Kazimiera M goes in the back of the room. Her brown hair, very tidy by now, cascades down her shoulders and her back.

Our photographs, our records. The first, the second, the next photograph. But how to record what happens in an instant? In an instant shorter than releasing the shutter? The movement of the goat's tail, which right away will hang still, the beating wings of Mr. Baum's pigeons, the watchman's hand rising behind the brewery gate, the butterfly flashing over the trees . . . Are those the records of one moment's events? Records or no records. Selected glimpses.

Although the all-seeing Eye of the Town, the dome of the Town Hall, doesn't take photographs, it sees everything all the time. Leybele, the Baums' oldest son, sits on the branch of the large horse-chestnut tree behind the school on Lwowska. He straddles the branch, holds a leaf in his teeth, looks ahead.

"But where are our boys?" Mrs. Zelda Baum looks up from the stove. Her husband, Hershe, has just entered the apartment. "I don't know where they are. I don't even know if they have eaten something. They didn't come to you at the store?" Mr. Hershe Baum shakes his head, takes off his vest, and hangs it on the chair. "They came to the store, but that was at noon. I gave them some money because they wanted to buy candy. I didn't see them later. Maybe they went to the meadows. . . . They go there every day. . . ." "They go there! Of course they go there! That's what a father says who doesn't know where his three sons are. And me? Am I supposed to know everything?" Although it isn't necessary, Mrs. Zelda Baum removes the stove lid and blows on the burning wood. Her wig has slid down the back of her head, ready to fall on the floor anytime now. "And I am supposed to know what to buy, where to be. And to mind all the children. Has it ever been different?"

Kazimiera M walks outside the house. She carries a plate full of strawberries. She approaches the lilac bushes that are out of bloom. She remembers the scent of their white and purple flowers. Lilacs bloom for a short time, a little over a week. May explosion. Then the flowers turn brown, as if tainted by rust. Kazimiera M keeps putting strawberries sprinkled with sugar into her mouth. Right behind her, at her heels, the goat follows. Its wet nose nudges the green dress with white flowers.

Here, among low apple trees, among lilac bushes, in the slender shadow of the pear tree, the air is more moist and possibly cooler. The leaves smell of pulsating juices.

An overturned tree trunk is under the lilac bush. Kazimiera M sits down on it. The goat has followed her here. It stands with its side turned toward Kazimiera M and looks at her. The goat is breathing deeply. Quiet puffing can be heard. The goat's belly is moving.

Kazimiera M sees the Baums' oldest son, Leybele, walking on Listopadowa from the vicinity of the flour mill.

Mr. Hershe Baum's pigeons are perching on the edge of the flat brewery roof. Others are flying there from the shed. The pigeon coop must be empty.

Holding a tin can in his hand, Mr. Hershe Baum stands in front of the shed. He looks at the brewery and whistles softly. He tosses wheat grain mixed with groat offal onto the roof of the shed. The pigeons land on the shed and raise their wings, trying to hoard as much grain as possible. We can hear their beaks striking the roof and the gentle tapping of their feet.

From behind the brewery gate, the dogs' barking has resounded.

There's grey smoke over the Baums' house. It goes up, to the receding sun, to the advancing stars. The smoke must veil the sky so that the evening can be beautiful, so that the stars can see themselves in the shiny skins of the cherries.

Leybele shuts the gate. Mr. Hershe Baum turns his eyes on him, forgetting the pigeons, which are waiting for the next portion of grain. "Where have you been, Leybele? What will you tell your mother? She hasn't seen you since morning and is very angry. Tell her you were over at your aunt's and you ate dinner there. Don't just stand there, go quickly in the house."

Attorney Walenty Danilowski wipes his wet body with a large white towel. His vigorously rubbed arms become flushed. He turns in front of the mirror. Water trickles along his back, down his buttocks and legs. From his chest and arms he moves the towel onto his back. He runs his hand over the steam-covered mirror.

Blended with the hot steam, the smell of lavender wafts in the bathroom. In June, likewise, hot steam, blended with the smell of simultaneously blooming herbs and grasses, wafts through the meadow air. Because June comes only once a year, the warmed-up meadow vegetates recklessly, impetuously, with every leaf counting the pieces of sun that keep falling from the sky. The attorney likes the atmosphere in the bathroom, the sweat flowing in large drops on his skin. A tiny window at the level of his head is closed. Steam covers the windowpane.

So—the steam. The meadow. The lavender. Attorney Walenty Danilowski has dried himself and again dips his arms in water. And instantly he submerges his head—as if he had submerged himself into the abyss of smell, into infinite greenness. Let things remain unchanged. The fifth, the tenth descent into Heraclitean waters.

The policemen, Antoni Wrzosek and Tomasz Romanowicz, are leaving the police station. The hands of the Town Hall clock have moved considerably—the time is 7:30. More sensitive mechanisms would inform us that it is 7:30 and 6 seconds, 7—now 8—seconds past 7:30. Does that have any significance for the policemen?

They are walking towards the Lvov Gate, toward the New Town. Their swift and rhythmic steps can be heard. Ahead of the policemen, the shadow that can't be overtaken moves together with them. They pass the linden trees outside Attorney Walenty Danilowski's office. They follow the footprints of the pious Hasidim. (Those tracks are a mystery that should be viewed from close quarters—bend your head, Tomasz, bend it lower. Those Hasidim belong to the incomprehensible that must be comprehended.) Did the policemen see them? Did they hear their singing?

"Why are we in a hurry? Wait, Antoni, it's half an hour till eight. We have time."

"Yes, we have time. We won't drink beer at Rosenzweig's until tomorrow. We'll never be late for that. How is your brother?"

In a few minutes the policemen will reach the Jewish cemetery. On the other side of the street, opposite the cemetery, they will pass a closed store with the sign GLASS. GLASS UTENSILS. Behind the store window they will see long, narrow jars and glass vases in various sizes. They won't hear the cooing of the wild pigeons. Looking at the Jewish cemetery, the policemen won't see anybody. Antoni Wrzosek will say, "I've often wondered what's written on those graves."

Musing over the unknown meaning of the Hebrew inscriptions, they'll pass the Jewish cemetery, Orla Street, and Saint Augustine's Church. Passing the church, they'll bend their heads, and they'll hear the organ. Its sound will follow them until they reach market square. There they will sit on the bench that stands on the square's western side near the wall of the wicker goods store.

What will be happening in the market square?

The officers will exit Rosenzweig's tavern. They will leave the uneaten scrambled eggs, half-empty wine glasses, and also the steins wet with beer foam. Before the door closes behind the last of the officers, Rosenzweig's wife, Cywia, will start collecting steins, glasses, and plates with leftover eggs. And the tavern owner will sigh with relief, glad that his customers are departing. The officers, tired of the daylong heat and the stuffiness in the tavern, will unbutton their uniforms. Outside the tavern, they will look around for a droshky. Unfortunately, only two wagons that belong to Rosenzweig's customers will stand in the market square. And not a trace of the droshky. Laughing loudly, and most indiscreetly making plans for the evening, the officers, stumbling along the pavement, will slowly come to the center of the market square. Here they will again look around in search of a carriage.

The moment the officers reach the intersection of Lwowska and Ogrodowa, several of Rosenzweig's pigeons will fly into the market square to peck at the grain scattered under the wagons in front of the tavern.

Unable to find a droshky, the officers will make up their minds to go to the Old Town on foot. "Don't they serve excellent wine in this tavern! . . . Who would have expected it!" one of the officers will remark when passing the wicker goods store. Antoni Wrzosek will quietly sigh in response.

Right at this moment the policemen's shadow will disappear. They will have passed the second corner of the store.

Soon afterwards the sound of the organ, reaching as far as the market square, will subside and, along with it, the singing of the choir will subside.

But that isn't happening yet. Now the policemen can still hear the organ and the choir. They can also hear the officers unsuccessfully calling the cab that is driving away on Gminna Street. And they can hear the clatter of the wheels and the clatter of the horses' hooves.

Sitting on the bench (Tomasz Romanowicz will light a cigarette), the policemen will also see that:

Rosenzweig's pigeons, having fed on the grain scattered under the wagons, will fly back to the pigeon coop.

The Baums' two daughters will enter the market square from Ogrodowa. The taller one, in a blue dress, will hold an orange-and-white kitten. Passing the fabric store, they will peek inside through the chinks in the shutters. They will leave the market square, taking the footpath that Roza took to Spadek. The sunflowers, facing west, will sway toward the policemen.

There is less sun. (Is that why there are fewer swallows over the town?)

At this time Mr. Antoni Wrzosek will look at his watch. It will show 7:55. By 8:00, they will also notice that:

One of the patrons will leave Rosenzweig's tavern. For a short time—a minute or even less—he will go behind the tavern and then return to the market square to his horses. After tightening the loose harness, he will get on the wagon. Cracking the whip, he'll say loudly to the horses, "Home, let's go." Dirt will rise from under the wheels and the hooves. (In fact it won't be only dirt but sundust as well. It seems that neither Rosenzweig's customer nor the policemen know about that.) The wagon will cut across the market square and disappear behind the houses on Lwowska.

The Town Hall clock and Antoni Wrzosek's watch show that it is past eight o'clock. The policemen get up from the bench.

"Leybele, go and look for the goat. It must be somewhere near the house. I heard it bleating a while ago." Leybele sits with his head bent down. Without looking up, he walks across the dirt and crumbled straw that his mother is sweeping. When he opens the door, the rush of air stirs up the shreds of straw.

Entering the street, Leybele kicks and crushes the apples lying in front of the house. The smell of the juice squirting from the apples permeates the air. Leybele picks up an apple, turns it in his fingers and examines it. He closes the gate, stops and tosses the apple as high as he can, following its course. With a dull thump, the apple falls on the brewery roof, rolls for a moment, slides down the wall and rolls on the grass, on Listopadowa.

Kazimiera M is no longer under the lilac bush. Perhaps she has gone back to her apartment and will soon appear in the window.

The goat stands under the lilac bush close to the trunk. Leybele breaks off a branch, strikes it on the rump, and prods it on. The goat takes a few steps but not in the direction of Listopadowa. Leybele grabs it by the ear and, walking ahead, pulls it behind himself.

By the time Leybele brings the goat to the shed and by the time Mrs. Zelda Baum squeezes out the first drops of goat milk, the following events will occur:

Kazimiera M will walk outside and gesture for the boy to come to her. The freed goat will go back under the lilac, but at the moment when Leybele comes to Kazimiera M, the goat nibbling on the grass will hide behind the bushes. Kazimiera M will give the boy three pieces of candy. She'll ask him to go and look for Romanowicz, the policeman, and tell him to come here in an hour or an hour and a half.

A white butterfly will fly over the tree.

Leybele's friends will come. Kazimiera M will return to her apartment, one more time urging Leybele not to forget her request. Leybele will share the candy with his friends—as it will turn out, the candy will have a fruit filling—and together they'll go inside Listopadowa, to the flour mill.

At the sight of the women returning from the market square, the dogs will bark behind the brewery gate.

Back from the flour mill, Leybele will look for the goat. Pulling it by the ear and hitting it with a branch, he'll lead the goat to the backyard where Mrs. Zelda Baum is waiting.

In the meantime a small group of people have an opportunity to see a meteorite tracing an arc in the sky, falling somewhere in the north, past the place where Listopadowa ends, past Hrubieszowska too. A photograph of a shining point will enrich our collection.

The dome of the Town Hall sees the place where the meteorite has fallen. Can anyone count its reflections in the shiny cherries? Are they a sign of something? What do they signify?

Right at the moment when the meteorite touches the ground,

the first drops of goat milk squeezed out by Mrs. Baum begin to fall. Mrs. Baum sits on a wooden stool near the doorstep to her house, holding a pot between her knees. When the milk squirts into the pot, it makes a metallic sound. At the bottom of the pot, a skin forms with bubbles of foam that burst instantly.

The drops of vodka fall that Rosenzweig's patron has shaken out of an empty glass. The patron grimaces after taking a gulp of strong liquor. Has he heard about phenomena such as the meteorite, about which little is known? Somewhat cheerless this evening, the patrons look dolefully at one another. It isn't yet time to go home. Not until tomorrow will they find out about the meteorite that traced a shiny arc in the sky.

A thin moon has appeared, perhaps thinner than the moons in Roza's ears. It hangs over the Labunka.

As is their habit, the policemen stroll along the edge of the market square. They haven't seen the meteorite, but they will hear about it, maybe even this day. Maybe they would have seen the meteorite in the skins of the cherries if they had picked them. But they didn't. That time can't be recovered. From behind the second-story window, they can hear a conversation. The pavement in the market square hasn't quite cooled off yet. It is warm—still warm. A cat can tread on it without fear.

Mrs. Zelda Baum has finished milking the goat. She tells her son to lock the goat in the shed. Leybele begs his mother to let him go to the market square for a while. He wants to see his friend. "You've had enough. Nobody knew where you were all day long. Lock the goat up and come home. Tomorrow you'll have time for your friend."

The goat leaps gingerly across the doorstep to the shed. Leybele throws a few crushed apples into the shed for the goat to munch on and fastens the door with a hasp. Above the goat, in the cage, the pigeons are cooing.

Behind the window of the Baums' house, Mr. Hershe Baum is visible in the light of a lamp. Mr. Baum is sitting over the Book spread out on the table. His head is bent, his temples rest on his hands, his lips move silently. The Word whose wisdom blinds like a closely observed meteorite.

The pipe of the Baums' cast-iron stove coughs today's last clouds of smoke. The white-grey smoke rises higher and higher. The smoke takes the place of the clouds that haven't been seen since morning. It floats south toward the outskirts of town and covers the motionless moon.

We can hear the bucket falling into a well, the clanging chain, the accelerating crank, and the protracted squeaking—or rather groaning—when the bucket ascends. But it isn't happening here. The sounds come from behind Lwowska, maybe from the other part of Listopadowa. A moment later we can hear water being poured from one bucket into another.

The tin chimney lets out less and less smoke—the white-grey trail looks like the steam that was sliding, if it was sliding at all, down the brewery roof. Now we can see the last gasps of the stove, weak as a breath on a freezing day. Mrs. Zelda Baum puts no more wood in the fire.

The clouds of smoke have veiled the moon. The skins on the cherries have stopped glistening. Was it then only the pale moonlight that transformed the cherries into jewels?

No one is behind the brewery gate. Listopadowa is deserted, the dogs don't bark. Watchful, they prick their ears, listening to the town's sounds. Maybe they hear the water that is being poured? Or maybe they hear the policemen's conversation?

The clouds of smoke, which up till now have been soaring over the Baums' house, over Listopadowa and the market square, vanish somewhere beyond Ogrodowa. Maybe the birds have scattered them like Mr. Baum's pigeons did this morning. The moon is visible once more.

In the moonlight, in the light of the setting sun, and also in the light of the glistening cherries, Kazimiera M can be seen flipping the pages of a book. Several illustrated journals and some women's magazines are lying on the table. Everything is strewn around and opened at random.

In Rosenzweig's tavern, three lamps are lit—one on the counter, two on the tables. Flickering brightness. The patrons' shadows shift on the walls.

Tired Rosenzweig—didn't he count the steins of beer, the herring fished out of the jar?—sits motionless behind the counter, staring at some point, with half-closed eyes, perhaps listening raptly to the rhythm of the ending day, perhaps calling up the faces of today's customers, perhaps casting the words he's heard today into new sentences. Who can say? It's sleepy and quiet in the tavern. Like Rosenzweig, those who remain in the tavern stare, but they stare at something else, listening raptly to a different rhythm—their own.

Behind the patrons' backs, the fiery ball burns in the picture painted on wood, sending sparks onto the floor and filling the tavern with them. Some of the people we saw soaring over the town with outstretched arms are already above the clouds. That happened after we looked at the picture the first time. Since then, the ball has rolled into the middle of the market square.

Three lamps wouldn't be enough to let us scrutinize Rosenzweig's face. The light from the fiery ball exposes the furrows symmetrically crossing his cheeks, a few short hairs, which have sprouted on his nose, and also his knit brows, their arches dropping steeply. The half-opened eyes close now and again, and the nostrils quiver. The words called back to mind have cast themselves into new sentences. Therefore: hush! Sit in silence, gentlemen. Don't ask for anything. If someone is overcome with sleep, let his head fall noiselessly on the table, on his outstretched hands. Let the sparks from the picture lighten up his sleep. (Maybe one of the patrons will dream of burning tar dropped from hell, sizzling as it falls toward the ground.)

If we could see into this dream, we would see the meteorite or burning tar. But who will try to understand what the dream means? Could it have meaning for anyone except the dreamer?

The still eye of the herring watches the tavern from behind the wall of the glass jar. Always wide open, turned toward Rosenzweig and at the same time toward the patrons, the penetrating eye takes in each corner, each movement of the leg under the table. It also sees that right below it, on the blue countertop, the drops of water and beer are drying, their meticulous design created by Rosenzweig's rag. The eye of the herring notices that Rosenzweig's eyelids drop and his head bends a few centimeters.

A customer stands up from a table nearest the door. The sound of the bench pushed along the floor wakes up Rosenzweig, who raises his head abruptly—all the time the eye of the herring is motionless—and opens his eyes wide. "Good-bye, Mr. Rosenzweig, time to go!" Through the crack in the open door, the eye of the herring looks at the market square. But it sees little: the store on the other side, the cooling stones, and the retreating leg of the customer hurrying to his horses.

The last wagon leaves from the tavern. ("What time is it, Mr. Rosenzweig?") The sky is clear of the white-grey smoke. The moon examines its reflection in the dome of the Town Hall, the all-seeing Eye of the Town.

When soon, walking on Spadek, Antoni Wrzosek and Tomasz Romanowicz pull on the branches of the cherry tree, the fruit they'll pick will blink in the darkness like tens of pairs of cats' eyes. Moonlight and the light of the first stars will be there. The sour juice will tickle Romanowicz's throat. Carelessly squeezed, it will flow down his hand, leaving a sticky reddish trickle.

Attorney Walenty Danilowski leaves his house without saying a word. The dazing and arousing smell of the roses stops him on the stairs. (Drawing the curtain aside, Mrs. Maria Danilowski looks from above.) Bees and bumblebees have flown off the roses. Penetrating the flower cups, they have undoubtedly opened the petals. Then, flying over the roses in front of the attorney's house, they carried this wonderful smell through the air. The attorney turns his head back, half closes his eyes. Another deep breath. The blood from his legs and arms flows toward his head. His fair hair—Walek's fair head—is among roses and other flowers. Under his feet, in the grass, some fallen petals. But not too many. Not all the roses and peonies have bloomed. Smaller and bigger buds. From some of them a petal or two or three uncertainly creep out. They must be helped, their blooming must be speeded up. Walek gently pulls the bud with his right hand toward himself, holding it at the base, and with his left hand strips the petals of their green covering. Now they can be opened one after another, one after another, the tenth, the thirteenth. At last—the whole peony blooms, no more buds remain. The next one must be helped. Walek's fair head among the clumps of flowers. He pulls off the green leaves that conceal the bud and begins to part the petals. (He has to squat, it'll be more comfortable that way.) "What are you doing there, Walek?" "I am—I am blooming!"

From the stairs the attorney steps down into the avenue. He plucks a few rose petals, puts them in his mouth, chews. The bitter-sour taste of the juice, a distinct hint of the familiar rose. And something like—maybe it's only an illusion, he isn't sure—something like the taste and smell of honey pollen. The time of opening the rosebuds, the time of blooming, was also the time of catching bees, of studying their anatomy as thoroughly as circumstances and his own inventiveness allowed; the time of pulling off their legs, seeking the pollen that they carried on their bodies. It was when he walked among the roses and opened them that he caught the bees strolling over the flower cups and removed the pollen with a blade of grass or his fingernail. The pollen tasted like rose petals—the taste and smell were almost the same—it tasted like the flowers from all over the garden. The pollen dissolved on the tongue like a drop—no, half a drop—of July honey. Did it hold the whole secret of the summer which he savored, recognized, and pondered, recalling the slightly forgotten scents and tastes of two or three years ago, though it seemed that those years couldn't be recaptured by memory? Or maybe it was only in tasting that he found the foretaste of mystery that was to be enacted in the autumn? The tongue sought the lines which once had described Walek's most intimate spaces, spaces that were within him—or more accurately, spaces that since then had been him. Which marked the most important contours of his interior landscape, when he last took in his mouth the pollen picked off the bees, the drop of July honey, so much like the pollen. This landscape couldn't be re-created in its former features, it couldn't be copied by anyone. How could something be re-created that he himself didn't quite know, that he had to try to recognize constantly and never with any certainty because everything that he already knew, everything that he could name only with difficulty, would continue to grow and reveal itself in an altered shape, iridescent with new colors? Is there then, in those yellow rose petals that the attorney is now chewing, something that could be compared to the previously savored secrets of the pollen? Can those lines be found which marked the attorney's most intimate landscape, created when he had no knowledge of their existence? The attorney spits out the chewed rose petals. They are now greenish, odorless pulp, incapable of calling up the time when Walek made the roses bloom. The attorney leaves the smell behind.

Turning his eyes toward the house, the attorney sees the dome of the Town Hall. From behind the houses and the trees, the Eye of the Town watches a curious microcosm, enclosed among the parted rose petals. Two kinds of beetles wander there—the black ones with tiny chitin wings and the hairy ones with a pair of prominent horns. Although it's getting dark, and little can be seen from such a distance, maybe the Eye of the Town will notice a stray bee ready to pass the night between two petals or under a leaf.

Attorney Danilowski looks at his watch. There's a droshky several steps behind him. The horse snorts. The attorney hails the droshky. "Where can I take you, Sir?"

The moon is more distinct. Its light, reflected in the cherries, is clearer now. The cherries also reflect the light of lamps that have been lit here and there. The cherries are lamps or stars lit for the benefit of the Eye of the Town so that it might peek among the rose petals (a few of the first stars, still barely visible, have just risen). Let's part the branches to see that light, to see closely the moon reflected in the cherries as if in a mirror. The day is ending, so let some of that light shine for the Book of the Day that is about to close.

The ducks from the park have hidden in the brake. The fish don't show their backs or snouts. The swallows have flown away from the park—they have returned to their nests or flown high into the unexplored spaces from which the meteorite fell. They have flown to the stars, flown to the moon, to be within its light and create new chapters of their own books.

A brown moth has fallen into the pond. Perhaps the light of the moon or of the stars reflected in the water has lured it. In confusion it is still moving its wings, more and more helplessly. The circles in the water spread irregularly. The stars shine on its surface. It doesn't take long. The moth stops moving. Maybe it's alive. The water calms. Together with the water, the light grows still.

Quiet gurgling. Every few seconds one bubble after another escapes to the surface and disappears, as if a hollowed-out stalk were discharging air under the water. Buzzing insects, chirping crickets. The air vibrates. From the islet the sound of a bird, long and rueful, rings.

(It's possible that the bird's voice signals the beginning of the last chapter of the Book of the Day.)

The policemen, Antoni Wrzosek and Tomasz Romanowicz, return to the market square from which they have been absent since the meteorite fell. They have appeared in the lane near Mr. Hershe Baum's fabric store. One of them—Wrzosek or Romanowicz? (they are the same height, and from this distance it's impossible to tell them apart)—one of them holds a branch broken off a fruit tree on Ogrodowa or Mlynska. They pick the fruit and put it in their mouths. Leaning against the wall of Mr. Baum's store, they look at the deserted market square. Before them, a few lights—in the windows of Rosenzweig's tavern and in some apartments. A distant train rumbles.

"What's going on over there?" Antoni Wrzosek points ahead with his hand. "Sparks are shooting up as if someone were sharpening a knife. Let's go and see." A dark grey cat, restlessly moving its tail, looks askance at the approaching policemen. If the encounter weren't unwelcome, the cat would continue shaking the sundust out of its coat. The cat lowers its head and vanishes noiselessly behind the store in the darkness of grass and burdock.

"So it's only a cat. And it seemed to me that I saw light." Antoni Wrzosek stops and stares into the trembling thicket. He would say more, but he can't find the words. The strangeness of the sundust falling out of the cat's coat allows no comment. He doesn't notice the blazing stones sprinkled with sundust, which in a moment will be extinguished forever. Tomasz Romanowicz doesn't see that. If asked, he wouldn't even be able to repeat what Antoni Wrzosek has been telling him.

The door to Rosenzweig's tavern squeaks. The light beam from the three lamps is cast onto the market square. In the light, the shadow of a patron leaving the tavern. The light beam didn't illuminate the policemen. The customer didn't even notice it.

A harmonica concert begins. Every day it plays Ukrainian tunes. It will play like that for about an hour. The policemen are used to it. A certain Wasyl (Antoni, what's his name, I keep forgetting . . .)—Czehyra. They need to get to Hrubieszowska—five minutes of a leisurely walk. That's where the music is coming from.

Again, the smell of rotting wood, of damp boards, more intense than in the morning. The death of houses and market stalls follows its own rhythm established through the years. For the present they are still alive.

A new star, infinitely small and barely visible. Can anyone see it?

In Rosenzweig's tavern, lights and shadows stir. It's the tavern owner: he has gone to the window and, shielding his eyes on both sides, looks at the market square and at the policemen. He raises his eyes to see the stars over the town. Time to close the tavern. The last patrons should have left forty-five minutes ago. They ate what there was to eat and drank what there was to drink. They talked—or rather kept silent. "Gentlemen, I have to close. Come back tomorrow. I wish you all good night."

The policemen are coming to Lwowska. We stood there in the morning taking the first photographs. Antoni Wrzosek shoves a bare branch behind the iron bar that locks the door to the soft-drink booth. The juice has ceased its assault on the leaves. The mystery of the roots is no longer transmitted into light. Romanowicz spits out the pit. It falls on the pavement under his feet and stops between two stones. Sand and sundust cling to it.

Now we can admire Antoni Wrzosek's beautiful mustache. Standing on the corner of the market square near the first house on Lwowska, he leans against a streetlamp. The sharp white light falls straight down and lets us see the pit. We can also see that the stones have completely cooled off. They are grey, pale grey, unlike the stones we saw in the afternoon—those were bright as the light of the streetlamp and dangerously hot. Mr. Antoni Wrzosek, his hands in his pockets, wonders where he can search for the explanation of the sparks. It can't be denied that those were sparks, this light resembling the sparks so much—which he just saw on the northern side of the market square. And that dark grey cat that ran into the grass, what could it have been doing near that light? Antoni Wrzosek's discreetly trimmed black mustache reaches halfway between the corners of his mouth and chin. The ends of his mustache curl up playfully. The foam from the beer, which tomorrow he will drink with Romanowicz at Rosenzweig's tavern, will settle on the mustache as if on the rim of a beer stein.

Tomasz Romanowicz squats before Wrzosek and picks his teeth with a splinter broken away from the branch. Several streetlamps on Lwowska are lit and Romanowicz can see into the street, but it is empty. Meanwhile, squeaking softly, the swinging door to Rosenzweig's tavern opens and closes. The door is pushed by the last patrons leaving the tavern. Like huge white wings, beams of light glide over the market square, pausing on the houses and the stores on the opposite side. We remember: three lamps, as well as the fiery ball in the picture, burn in the tavern. Antoni Wrzosek can see them because the light falls on him and also on Tomasz Romanowicz. The patrons' shadows grow unreal in size, only to disappear when the door closes. They reappear when it opens.

The harmonica is heard. The patrons, who are scattered over the market square, gracelessly attempt to pick up Wasyl's song, which dominates the music of the harmonica.

Rosenzweig blows out the flames in two lamps. The third lamp is still lit, and the eye of the herring notices an object left on the table by one of the patrons. Finally Rosenzweig blows out the flame of the third lamp, which stands on the counter near the jar of herring. He gropes for the doorknob on the kitchen door. He will return to the front of the store to close the shutters and fasten padlocks on the doors. But the eye of the herring won't see that. The tavern is dark, and a bay leaf will get in the way of the herring's vision.

It's impossible to predict where Rosenzweig's customers will go. Only a few are still in the market square, loitering and yelling. We would have to look for the rest of them in lanes, near store walls, perhaps on Gminna. The Eye of the Town will know best.

From Spadek, from the direction of Hrubieszowska, a droshky with the attorney in it drives up to Kazimiera M's house. The light in Kazimiera M's room is dimmed, so she must be at home. The attorney pays the fare and wishes the cabman good night. Damp lilac branches, damp grass. He shoves away the dew-covered branches that are brushing against his temples. From behind the brewery gate, dogs are barking at him. A curtain has stirred upstairs. For a moment Kazimiera M's face is visible in the window. The floor and the steps squeak as the attorney climbs upstairs to the second floor.

The policemen have left the place under the streetlamp. Walking on Lwowska, they pass Spadek. Right at this moment, the droshky drives into Lwowska from Spadek, and the two men have to quicken their pace to avoid startling the horses or falling under their hooves. The cabman bows to Antoni Wrzosek and Tomasz Romanowicz. He turns toward the Old Town.

When the droshky comes within the light of a streetlamp, the hair on the black horses glistens.

"Could it be the attorney going to see Kazimiera? We could have asked the cabbie, but now it's too late."

"Soon we'll find out. Maybe the curtains won't be closed?" Tomasz Romanowicz has just stopped cleaning his teeth and flicked the splinter away. "Are we going straight or turning onto Listopadowa?"

"However you want. We may turn onto Listopadowa." Before the policemen approach Listopadowa, the droshky will stop at the market square. Two of Rosenzweig's customers will noisily get into the droshky and tell the cabman to drive them to another restaurant. When the droshky starts moving, the policemen will be five steps away from Listopadowa.

Those five steps to be heard when the heels kick the pavement. To be seen. Five steps, five words for the Book. Gone. What's gone? Does everything pass? To save, but how? For whom? Before it is irretrievably lost, before it sinks into nonbeing, into eternal oblivion. The five steps that have been taken. The smoke scattered by swallows and pigeons. The burned paper that has settled on leaves, that has fallen into the grass. The afternoon sun suspended above the pear tree. The white butterfly soaring over it. Before everything is fulfilled. The sundust pouring down on the town. The seen or unseen couple. The deserted Jewish cemetery. What can be saved before all is fulfilled?

The policemen have turned onto Listopadowa. The cabhorses' hooves strike the pavement in the market square. The policemen can hear them. Tomasz Romanowicz has stumbled on a discarded wooden board—when that happened, a star flickered, yet it continues to shine. They walk in the direction where earlier in the evening the meteorite fell. They won't find it in the meadows or in the fields where it is now cooling off. They'll pass the brewery, the Baums' house, Kazimiera M's house, and the flour mill. Later they'll turn into Polna.

Before Mr. Hershe Baum, in his dream, enters the waters of the flood, before he soars over the town, enveloped by fire, he will turn several pages in the Book that is spread out in front of him. (That will happen in an hour or two, after he turns off the lamp and checks to see if the door is fastened with a hasp.) Wearily bowing his head before the lamp, so that the letters blurring in his eyes will stay distinct, he will move his lips, like now, soundlessly. Is there greater bliss than when the Book blinds with every Word and when the Light is never enough? The sons and the daughters are asleep. Mrs. Zelda Baum sighs in her sleep. A moth flies over the Talmud.

In the Baums' shed the goat groans. The light from the lamp in front of Mr. Baum shines into the shed through the cracks between the boards. Through the hole in the knot, we may peer inside the shed.

Looking stealthily behind the brewery gate, we can see two pairs of small lights, immovable, turned toward the stars, toward us, piercing the darkness.

Dew has appeared on the grass in front of the brewery. It's so abundant that it seems as if all the steam that slid down the roof today had turned into water or as if it had just rained heavily.

Before the policemen, who are now walking down Listopadowa, find themselves opposite the pear tree between the Baums' house and Kazimiera M's—that will happen in two or three minutes because the policemen aren't in a hurry—Rosenzweig will go from Gminna into the market square outside his tavern. Maybe he won't be seen by anybody. He will carefully close the shutters and fasten the swinging door with an iron bar and a padlock. In the tavern steeped in darkness, the eye of the herring will look from inside the jar. It will witness the fiery ball, from the picture hanging above the table, roll onto the floor and strew a thousand sparks. Or rather it will itself break into sparks, because once it touches the floor, it will disappear, and the tavern will become brighter. The bay leaf, which a moment ago floated in front of the eye of the herring, has settled at the bottom of the jar among the wild mustard seed. The sparks from the fiery ball are like the sundust in the market square at noon.

Mumbling something to himself, Rosenzweig, his head bent down, walks behind the tavern.

A cat watched the tavern owner's actions. The same cat that Antoni Wrzosek saw shaking sundust out of its coat and disappearing in the grass behind the store. So Rosenzweig wasn't unobserved. Although the market square was empty, the cat watchfully followed his every movement.

All of that happened in two minutes because the policemen have reached the pear tree. Two pairs of small lights have sprung up from behind the brewery gate. The baying dogs are storming the gate. The cat from the market square can surely hear the noise. Tomasz Romanowicz picks up an apple and hesitates. Should he throw it at the dogs or take a bite? We wish we could see his hand at the moment of hesitation. He raises the apple to his mouth and bites.

"I wonder if the attorney is at Kazimiera's? Nothing can be seen behind those curtains."

"Maybe something could be heard."

Simultaneously, both men laugh.

Mr. Hershe Baum turns a page in the Book. He rubs his eyes to keep at bay the overpowering desire to sleep. (It's hard to say if the effects of this act will last long. Mr. Hershe Baum repeats the action many times.) Sometimes a wing or an abdomen of a moth burning in the flame of the lamp will sizzle. The buzzing in the temples, the circulation of blood and thoughts. This buzzing becomes pain that can't be subdued. Mr. Hershe Baum massages his temples with his fingers. This action brings only temporary relief. The pain returns, as intense as before.

Behind Mr. Baum's back, the cast-iron stove is cooling off. An occasional, barely audible crackling—maybe wood that has turned to ash is breaking—reminds us that smoke was rising out of the pipe (which we can see above the roof) attached with copper wire to the wall. Mr. Hershe Baum doesn't have his vest on—the last gasp of the fire warms up his back. Over the Talmud a yellow flame explodes before his face.

When the flame flickers in the glass globe, slightly blackening its neck, Mr. Hershe Baum's shadow begins to rock. Lying on the pages of the Book, the fingers of his right hand, long and thin, close and open. The shadow stops moving when the flame grows longer, burning the remains of the moth.

In the bright light of the flame shining on the shed, we can see the Baums' goat lying on the straw, its neck outstretched. Its white spots let us picture the shape of its body in the darkness.

Leybele has said something in his dream. The overheard words and syllables don't form a comprehensible whole. Mr. Hershe Baum can understand only two words: *policeman* and *candy*. Who knows what they are supposed to mean? It seems that Leybele has said something about Kazimiera M, but that is rather doubtful, even unlikely. At the Baums' she isn't a topic of conversation. Mrs. Zelda Baum forbade the children any contact with her. After Leybele says, "The policemen in the market square," he covers his head with a pillow and grows silent. Mr. Hershe Baum turns his face back to the Book.

The sour smell of apples, mixed with the scent of stock and sunflowers, floats in the air.

Wasyl's concert ends when the policemen pass the brewery gate.

Attorney Walenty Danilowski begins to take off Kazimiera M's second garter. Kneeling down to make his task easier and to allow himself an opportunity to kiss Kazimiera M behind the knee (we ought to know that this is one of the attorney's favorite places; another is the crook of the elbow), he slowly pulls down the purple garter ornamented with blue and red roses in alternating rows. Kazimiera M remembered to put the garters on when she was getting ready for Tomasz Romanowicz's visit ("Why hasn't he come?"). He once confided to her that thighs adorned with garters looked ravishing. She carefully selected the pair most suitable for this evening. Fortunately, the attorney, whom she met last spring, has tastes quite similar to the tastes of her other clients or friends, so the trouble of putting the garters on was worthwhile. Her left leg bent at the knee and thrust forward, she stands before the attorney and waits until he gently lifts her foot and slides the garter off. After moving the garter one or two centimeters down, he moves it back, imperceptibly, to its previous place, busily nibbling her skin and pulling on her few hairs. Kazimiera M would like this protracted ritual to be over. In the meantime, she balances her weight on her right leg, from which the garter has already been removed. She closes her eyes—who knows what, or rather, who she is thinking of? She puts her fingers in the attorney's hair and moves them in circles. The attorney, stripped of jacket and shirt, bends over her knee, one hand fiddling with the garter, the other moving up, the fingers clutching the thigh and part of the buttock. Because the lamp that stands in the corner gives too little light, the attorney can't properly see the white-pink skin of her untanned legs or that of the rest of her body. But he is able to imagine the exact tone of her skin. We should know that the hue of the legs, of the whole woman's body, kindles powerful emotions within the attorney. Kazimiera M isn't even aware of that. Noted for her willfulness and playfulness, she might get tanned, not suspecting how much of her perverse charm would be lost on the attorney. For instance, Romanowicz doesn't seem to attach any significance to that, though, who knows, perhaps a beautiful tan (he boasts of one himself) would be more appropriate at this time of year. Anyhow, it's only a trifle.

Take, for instance, those hairs growing near her nipples, which, if Romanowicz is to be believed, are so attractive. Because of Romanowicz, Kazimiera M resists plucking them. (There are also a few hairs between her breasts—Romanowicz said something about them too—but right now they can't be seen.) Who knows what the attorney thinks about those hairs? It seems as if he remembered them when he was trying to pull them with his mouth, but it may have been accidental. Meanwhile, the attorney has slipped the garter several centimeters down and it may be assumed that soon he'll take it off. Besides, Kazimiera M's right leg has gone numb as a result of her standing in an uncomfortable position. She would be glad if the attorney quickly took the garter off. Slightly annoyed with this excessively drawn-out situation, only now does she notice the scent of lavender that surrounds them. With her left hand she takes hold of the attorney's chin, pulling him up and drawing his face away from her leg. With her right hand she grasps the garter, and lifting her leg, takes it off. She smiles at the attorney, kisses his cheek and his chin. She squats and embraces his back and neck. Between him and her lies the garter, of no more use today.

The policemen are coming close to Polna. They are opposite the house that has its eastern wall overgrown with grapevines. Like the Baums' children, the policemen will pull on the vines heavy with juice, sweetness, and sun, and pick the ripe grapes.

But before that the planets have to change their constellations several times, the sovereign reign of Cancer has to be completed—through Leo, Virgo, and Libra, whose coming is to be expected toward the end of September. And in the time of Cancer, Leo, Virgo, the sundust must fall, as it always falls at that time. And the pear tree between the Baums' and Kazimiera M's houses must bow its branches heavy with fruit and full of the heat of the sun, of its shattered rays that cover the leaves so that in one moment, unerringly predicted by the stars, the dust can alter the color of the leaves from green to yellow, to brown-red.

The policemen walk toward Spadek on Polna. Dust is kicked up from under their shoes and gathers on the grass growing on the side of the street, on the shoes that kicked it, on the plants. In a few minutes, they will be in front of Kazimiera M's house. Tomasz Romanowicz will draw to himself a branch of a cherry tree and pick the fruit for himself and for Antoni Wrzosek. "Look, Antoni, only a few steps away," he'll say. Romanowicz will tell him to wait in the market square, near the stalls, for an hour or an hour and a half. Parting the branches of the lilac bush, he'll take the path to Kazimiera M's. We won't witness the events that will take place after Romanowicz enters her apartment. Later, that is, in a little while, in the market square, he'll dismiss Wrzosek's questioning with suggestive silence.

In the distance, where the meteorite fell into a field of grain, a rushing, rumbling train stops. The trail of sparks shoots up, hissing, into the darkness. For a moment the figure of the engineer becomes visible. Standing in the back of the engine, he waves a lighted lantern over his head. The boxcars carry huge logs hewn in the forests of Zwierzyniec—a priority shipment to Lvov. The sparks flying over the cars vanish, die down, leaving not even a faint trace.

That trail of sparks, irretrievably vanishing in our eyes, will shoot up again many more times, though at another place, at another hour, over another train. But knowing the truth about the time that is called past, we know that also those other trails of sparks, rising in the darkness, seen or unseen, like the sundust noticed by only one of the policemen, will vanish in our memory. For its own sake our memory determines the hierarchies of what is or isn't worth remembering. Those hierarchies are illusory, and our knowledge of their meaning is never complete. Yet the pain is always the same because we have managed to save barely a fraction of events happening simultaneously. Events that will never again occur surrounded by details which exist only once during a particular constellation. Only an unyielding belief that we'll be able to bring to light some forgotten detail—the color of the sky on a July day in 1934, the taste of mints that someone was sucking, the shape of a mirror framed in carved wood, the first few wrinkles on the temples of one Kazimiera M, who unexpectedly left the town without letting anyone know, and many other small details, like the moon-shaped earrings of Roza, the Gypsy woman, which were designed to hang from her ears and glitter at that time and place—makes us search and probe the time that, like those earrings, those sparks over the train, is irretrievably lost.

The Book of the Day has been written. Stars twinkle on the skins of sour cherries. Some wane. Others rise. If someone wanted to write their Book, he could begin the way we did: We are on Listopadowa.